CHEERLEADERS FROM PLANET

J÷M÷J

CHEERLEADERS FROM PLANET 

LYSSA CHIAVARI

Kraken
Collective

for my sisters: by chance and by choice

- Chapter 1 -

I looked up from my phone at the sound of wheels on asphalt. Not car wheels. Smaller, like the wheels on a skateboard. But they were moving fast, way faster than a skateboard should. Hella fast.

A second later, she came into view. I blinked to make sure I wasn't imagining things, but nope. She was really there. A cheerleader on a skateboard. She glided with the momentum of someone careening down a steep hill—something we didn't exactly have a shortage of here in the outer peninsula—her strawberry-blond ponytail streaming defiantly out behind her, as if she were daring the universe to make her regret going that fast without a safety helmet.

And if the sight of a cheerleader on a skateboard *in her uniform* hadn't been one of the weirdest things I'd seen in my nineteen years, what she did next clinched it. When she got to the bottom of the hill—right at the part of the street where I always got nervous because there was no guardrail and the road curved around a drop-off to the valley a few hundred feet below—she did a trick. Like one of those ones you see the guys in the skate park do, where they flip their boards up and do a spin? Only she wasn't in a skate park. She was on the freaking street, just inches away from a gorge that I was sure had to have claimed numerous lives in vehicular accidents.

I nearly had a heart attack just watching her, but the cheerleader was unfazed. She landed neatly on her board and kept right on going, the grin on her face wide, speeding along down the road like it was no big thing. My eyes followed her as she disappeared around the corner.

When I finally found my voice again, I turned to my uncle Tonio, who was sitting next to me on the bench outside the train station. "Did you see that?"

He looked up from his own phone. The sun glinted off the top of his bald scalp—with his shaved head and earring, I always thought my uncle looked like a Filipino version of Mr. Clean. "See what?" he asked.

"That girl on the skateboard!" I rolled my eyes at his blank expression. "Come on," I groaned. "Blond girl? Cheerleader? She did, like, a 360-fakie ollie or whatever the hell they call them."

Tonio chuckled. "I wish I'd seen that. Did her skirt go up?"

There was a crunching sound in my ears. I realized after a moment that it was the sound of me grinding my teeth. My family had a way of doing that to me. Especially my uncle Tonio. He was my mom's youngest brother, who lived at my parents' ranch along with them, my grandma, and (occasionally, now that I was in college) me. And he was only ten years older than me—old enough that he'd always seemed like a grown-up to me, but young enough that he still *acted* like a kid.

"I didn't see," I said, my face hot. He gave me a look that clearly said, "*I don't believe you.*" I glared and added, "She had on those little shorts they wear underneath. And you're gross."

Tonio laughed, his voice echoing across the street and over the gorge. "You're the gross one, looking at high school girls."

"She wasn't a high school girl," I said defensively. "Her uniform said *Swordsmen* on it. That's Bayview's mascot." Bayview University was the rival of my own college, St. Francis. Their campus was in City West. I wasn't much into sports, but it was hard to exist on campus without hearing about the rivalry between the Mariners and the Swordsmen.

"Bayview?" Tonio said, screwing up his face. "The hell's she doing out here in Everett?"

I shrugged. "Maybe she has family here or something. I think their spring break is the same time as ours."

Tonio looked dubious. I knew what he was thinking—no self-respecting Everett kid would go to Bayview. But he was prejudiced, being a St. Francis alum himself.

I shrugged and stood up. "I should probably get going, anyway," I said. "My train should be coming in any time. Thanks for the ride."

He nodded and stood up, handing me my overnight bag. "I'm glad you were able to come home for a little bit," he said, sounding sheepish. He wasn't usually one to get sappy, but he always got like this whenever I headed back to school, even though I was only an hour away from home. "See you next month for Easter?"

I laughed, leaning over to hug him. "Of course."

I was still grinning as I entered the station, swiping my Peninsula Rapid Transit pass through the reader on the turnstile. It was Thursday—I still had four days left of spring break, so I technically didn't need to head back just yet. But I still had to write a paper for my English class and come up with a presentation for Public Speaking, one of the horrible G.E.s that St. Francis made us take our freshman year. And the chances of getting any work done at home were slim to none.

Especially this week. My cousin Carmen had gotten married on Saturday, and the reception had been at my parents' house. Tons of family members had flown in for it—never underestimate the size of a Filipino family—and half of them seemed to be planning on staying for the indefinite future. There wasn't a quiet corner to be had in the whole house.

And then there was the baggage that weddings always seemed to bring out. It had started at the reception on Saturday night. My grandma had said, in a voice loud enough that our neighbors two miles down probably heard it, "Now the only one left is Laura." (That's me.) "When are you going to find a husband, Leelee?" (That's also me—don't ask.)

I'd frozen in the middle of a bite of puto. Then I glared at her. My lola had lived with us long enough to know better than to ask a question like that.

Fortunately, my mom came to my rescue. "Now, Mama," she said, "you know Laura doesn't date men—"

"Fine, then," Lola interrupted, undaunted. "When is she going to find a *wife?* I want some grandchildren!"

I choked down the sweet lump of rice cake in my

mouth. "Lola, I *am* your grandchild! And before you even start, you already have three great-grandkids." I pointed violently in the direction of my cousin Nina and her husband, accidentally smacking Tonio across the chest in the process. "What more do you want? Besides, I'm not even the last one. What about him? He's almost thirty!" I jabbed my finger into Tonio's chest again.

"Damn, woman, watch where you point that thing," he complained, rubbing his sternum.

"We're not talking about Tons," my grandma replied. (Seriously, just don't ask.)

"That's not fair!" I protested. "Why should he get off the hook because he's a guy? What is this, the Middle Ages?"

Lola merely narrowed her eyes at me. That was enough to make me sit down and shut up. That woman was like a demon lord in a tiny body. She was less than five-feet tall, but I swear, she would have left those giant pro-wrestlers she was always watching on TV quaking in their boots.

And that had been it. The whole rest of the week— what was supposed to be my spring vacation, I might add—had been spent trying to deflect the *"When are you going to get married?"* demands from my entire extended family. No one seemed to care about the fact that I was only *nineteen*, or that I'd only been out of high school for less than a year.

"This is all your fault," I'd said to my dad last night, flopping into the overstuffed armchair in his office. "You married into this."

Dad just looked up from his computer—he'd been working on something that involved way too many spreadsheets; you'd be surprised how much math ranching involves—and laughed, running a fair hand through his honey-brown hair. I knew what he was thinking. He was an only child, and both of his parents had been only children as well. He *liked* my mom's crazy enormous family, and how different they were from his own.

Well, honestly, I did too. But not when they were being pains in the ass like they were this week. Which is why I'd decided to go back to campus early. Well, that and the fact that my stomach couldn't take much more fried food. My mom and grandma had been making lumpia every day *"since we have company."* Never mind the fact that the company seemed intent on becoming permanent house guests.

I'd almost forgotten about the girl on the skateboard by the time my train pulled into the station. I was alone on the platform apart from a middle-aged couple; not too many commuters were heading into the City on a Thursday afternoon. I settled into a seat near the back of the train, a front-facing one since I always got motion sickness if I faced rear. The couple from the platform boarded the same car as me, and they sat closer than I would have liked, considering that the car was empty. I hoped they didn't want to socialize. Train conversations were always awkward enough, but I was still burned out from five days with my relatives. I slipped in my earbuds quickly and looked resolutely out the window, hoping to ward off any attempts at chitchat. It would be a good hour and a half to my final stop in City East, since I had to make a transfer partway through. Theoretically, it would be quicker by car, but traffic going in and out of the City was always terrible, no matter what time of day it was, and there was never any parking, anyway. Growing up on the peninsula, I'd gotten used to going everywhere by train.

It was actually pretty quiet until we got about five minutes away from my transfer. I was zoning out, my face rested against the glass of the window as I stared down at my phone, when I caught movement out of the corner of my eye. I glanced up. An oncoming train leaving the San Luis station headed back out toward Everett was approaching on the other track. I almost looked down again, but then a flash of light from the other train made me freeze. It looked like lightning, except there wasn't a cloud in the sky.

Oh, and, of course, it was *red*.

I kept my eyes riveted on the train, sure I must have been seeing things. But as the two trains drew closer to each other, I realized that I most definitely hadn't imagined it. Something was happening on that train—though I couldn't quite say *what*.

There was a figure on the roof. I didn't understand how there *could* be, considering how fast the trains were moving, but there he was, black trenchcoat flapping in the wind like a character from the freaking *Matrix* or something.

And then, in a flurry of movement, another figure darted up from the side of the train farthest from mine. She landed in a red blur on the roof in front of Mr. Trenchcoat. Her strawberry-blond ponytail whipped around her head frantically in the powerful wind.

It couldn't be.

The skateboarding cheerleader.

I only saw her for a split second as my train tore past hers. I gasped and jumped to my feet, pressing my hands against the window and craning my neck to try to see more. She rushed at the guy, and it looked like she was going to punch him, but then another figure obscured my view. I blinked in surprise and found *another* freaking cheerleader in front of me, clinging to the side of the other train right alongside my window. I couldn't even tell what she was holding on to; she was just *stuck* there like a damn lizard or something. She looked at me for just a second, her pale green eyes seeming to register in a lightning-fast instant that I had seen her. Then she was gone, ripped from my view by the movement of the trains.

I whirled around, yanking my earbuds out of my ears in a frenzied motion. The middle-aged couple stared at me like I was bonkers. "Are you okay?" the taller man asked.

"Did you see that?" I croaked.

"See what?" the shorter man said. I could barely see the movement of his mouth behind his bushy mustache.

"The cheerleaders! On the roof of the other train!" Even as I said it, I realized how crazy I sounded. And there I'd been, the one trying to avoid weirdos on the train.

"I didn't see anything." The mustachioed man chuckled nervously, scooting closer to his partner while simultaneously trying to make it look like he wasn't.

Their reaction was like a splash of cold water. I ran a hand through my hair in an attempt to calm my erratically-beating heart and managed an awkward grin. "Sorry," I said. "I think I must have been dozing. I talk in my sleep sometimes."

I didn't talk in my sleep—to my knowledge, anyway—and I definitely hadn't been dozing, either. But the couple seemed reassured by my words. They laughed easily, relaxing visibly. I laughed along with them, sinking back into my seat and putting my earbuds back in. The other train was long out of sight now, and the blinking L.E.D. sign at the front of the car indicated that we'd be pulling in to the San Luis station, where I needed to make my transfer, in two minutes. I could take care of everything then. These random strangers might not believe me, but PeRT security would be another story.

- Chapter 2 -

Or so I thought.

Seeing the security guard's face as I told him my story, I realized that maybe going to the cops wasn't the best idea I'd ever had. He looked like he thought I was even crazier than the couple on the train had.

"Cheerleaders," he repeated. "On the roof of a moving train."

"And a guy in a trenchcoat," I added.

"Right. Of course. And what were they doing there, exactly?"

I let out an exasperated sigh. "How should I know? Pulling a prank, probably." Or getting into a gang fight, I thought, remembering the way the blond girl had charged Mr. Trenchcoat. "They were moving too fast for me to ask their motives. But shouldn't you let the train operator know? I don't think PeRT will be too happy if someone dies or something, falling off the roof of one of their trains."

He looked at me hard for a minute, and I thought he was going to dismiss me. But then he nodded. "All right. I'm going to get one of my supervisors. Wait here, please, Miss—?"

"Clark," I said. "Laura Clark. Thanks." I flashed him my most appreciative smile. "I won't move a muscle."

I stood back against the heavily-graffitied concrete wall and watched the officer until he disappeared through a door on the other side of the crowded station. A clock above the door showed that there were fifteen minutes until my train was due. I hoped security was quick enough that I wouldn't miss it.

"I don't know where the hell they could be," a girl's voice near me snapped, jarring me out of my thoughts. I glanced absently in her direction and did a double-take. It wasn't just that she was gorgeous, which I would have had to be blind to miss. It was what she was wearing.

A Bayview University cheer uniform.

She wasn't the only one, either. A group of six other girls stood alongside her, all clad in the same red-and-silver getup, a pirate's sword appliqued across the front. What was this, a damn cheerleader convention?

"Try calling them one more time," said a petite girl with black hair twisted into dozens of braids. "They should be here by now."

The first girl who'd spoken made a noise of annoyance and turned on her heel, storming in my direction. My heart staggered for a minute, but she brushed past without even looking at me, staring down at her phone. She swiped her thumb across it a couple of times, then lifted it to her ear. I watched her self-consciously. Her dark waist-length hair was pulled into a half-up, half-down style, and the upper portion was curled and streaming with silver and red ribbons. With her lithe, athletic figure and flawless porcelain skin, she made a picture-perfect ambassador for Bayview. Hell, forget head cheerleader—she could have been queen of the school.

Except for that scowl on her face, of course. Pretty sure the cheer coach at my old high school would have slapped any of her girls she caught wearing an expression like that. Nothing but a Barbie-like grin would fly for that squad. I'd never even bothered to try out. My best attempt at a phony smile just looked like I was smelling something bad.

"Leah, where the hell are you?" the girl suddenly snapped into her phone. She was pacing back and forth in front of the wall a few feet away from me. She glanced blankly in my direction for a second, her brown eyes locking with mine. A weird feeling washed over me, like déjà vu. She reminded me of someone—a girl I'd had a crush on in middle school, I think. I couldn't remember her name for the life of me, though. "You and Joanie were supposed to meet us at San Luis half an hour ago. If your asses don't get here in five minutes, we're going to be late for the meet. So freaking call me already."

She hung up, turning in my direction again. I didn't realize I'd been staring at her until suddenly she was staring—scowling—back.

"Hey," she said, and I felt panic rear up inside me. I was already mentally preparing my excuses for the *"What are you looking at?"* that was sure to follow, but she shocked me by instead saying, "Do I know you?"

"Uh, I don't think so," I said quickly, even though I'd been wondering the same thing. I didn't remember much about that girl from middle school, but if this *was* the same girl, I definitely didn't want her to remember me. My braces and outdated glasses had been the least embarrassing things about me back then. "But I couldn't help but overhear— you're missing a few of your friends? I think I might have seen them."

That made her eyebrow go up. "You? Where did *you* see

them?"

I ignored the loaded way she said *you* and replied, "I saw a blond girl wearing a uniform like yours in Everett earlier. And then on the train—" I broke off. Actually, that was yet another weird thing about the entire incident. I'd seen her on her skateboard in Everett, but then fifteen minutes later she'd been on a train heading back *toward* Everett. How had she gotten there so fast?

The girl didn't notice the confusion on my face, though. She was looking off in the direction of the train platforms, her scowl deepening. "Everett?" she murmured. "What was she...?" She looked back at me. "Damn. Listen—"

She broke off suddenly, whirling around. The security guard I'd spoken to earlier was coming back out of the office, followed by another officer with stripes on his sleeves.

The cheerleader cursed. "They've noticed us. We need to get out of here."

I furrowed my eyebrows. "Why? They're just coming over to talk to me. I...I needed to tell them something."

She glared at me. "About Leah?"

I just gaped back at her. What was *with* these cheerleaders?

"Shailene!" The girl with the braids was hurrying toward

us. "Sentries."

"I see them," the one who'd been speaking to me—Shailene, I guess—said. "We need to get out of here. And that includes her." She pointed at me.

"Who's she?" the other girl asked.

"Laura," I said after a minute, realizing they were waiting for a response. I don't think that was the answer they wanted, though.

"She *saw* Leah," Shailene said. "In Everett."

The other girl cursed now. "Okay. We'll distract the sentries, then. You get her out of here."

"Um, I'm not going anywhere," I interrupted, jerking my arm away when Shailene reached for it. "I have to catch my train. I don't have time for kidnapping-by-cheerleader, thanks."

I turned on my heel, striding confidently toward the two security guards, who were pushing forcefully through the crowd. I'd only made it about three steps, though, when a redheaded cheerleader whipped past me—way faster than I would have thought was physically possible, even for someone fit enough to hoist a fully-grown human on her shoulders. She held something black and metallic in her right hand. For one horrible instant, I thought it was a gun; I realized what it *actually* was just half a second before she pulled the trigger. Barbs shot from the barrel, careening toward the officer faster than my eyes could keep up, and then electricity crackled through the air.

"Are you freaking nuts?" I shrieked. "You can't just *tase* the cops!"

The cheerleader ignored me. The security guard cried out in pain, staggering backward into the other officer—but he wasn't a cop anymore, I realized with horror. As the electricity pulsed through the security guard's body, it shimmered, and the human appearance seemed to fall away like shredded clothing. What was left was... I don't even know what it was, honestly. The closest description I could come up with was a giant black pincher bug on two legs.

I screamed bloody freaking murder.

"Come on," Shailene barked, and this time I ran after her without hesitation. I hadn't thought I would see anything weirder today than these cheerleaders, but at least they were human. I think.

We raced up the stairs to the train platforms, Shailene leading the way. "What the hell was that thing?" I panted. "And why doesn't anyone else see it?" After the Taser incident, I'd have thought for sure that the station would be pandemonium, but the only person screaming had been me—and no one seemed to have noticed that, either.

"They're Anesidorans," Shailene called over her

shoulder. "And no one can see them because they don't *want* to be seen." She ducked under a metal guardrail with a sign attached to it that read *No Admittance,* and crouched behind the controller box.

"What the hell does that mean?" I asked, following her. "Just *wanting* to be invisible doesn't *make* you invisible." I of all people ought to know that, considering how many times I—with or without my family's help—had managed to mortify myself in public. But I kept that addendum to myself.

Shailene rolled her eyes. "It is *way* too complicated to explain right now. All I want is for you to tell me where you saw Leah and Joanie and then to get the heck out of here before those sentries find us."

"I told you, I saw the blond girl in Everett. And then..." I swallowed at the memory of the second incident. It seemed a lot more sinister now, after seeing that bug monster down there. "I saw her and another cheerleader on a train heading *toward* Everett. They were on the roof of the train. And there was a guy with them, a guy in a black trenchcoat."

Shailene's already-pale skin went white as a sheet. She'd pulled two tripod-looking devices from...somewhere (did cheerleader uniforms usually have pockets? Where would they *fit?*), and she froze in the middle of unfolding the legs of the second one. "Goddammit," she muttered.

"What? What's the matter?"

She glared at me. "Don't worry about it. It just means I need to get you out of here before—"

She broke off. The officer with the stripes on his sleeves had appeared at the top of the stairs. He *looked* human, but after seeing what had happened with his buddy downstairs, I somehow got the feeling that he *wasn't*.

"Hold still," Shailene whispered. Hurriedly, she unfolded the legs of the second tripod and set it down on the other side of me. Then she pressed a button on the base of each and some kind of digital screen shimmered into place in front of us.

"Anesidoran sentries don't *see* the way we do," she explained in a low voice. "That should scramble his vision sensors enough that he won't find us. Hopefully."

"*Hopefully?* And what do we do if he does find us?" I couldn't believe that he wouldn't be able to see right through this mostly-transparent screen. And what about the other passengers at the station?

"You don't want to find out," Shailene said.

I ground my teeth. As if that weren't the most contrived action-movie response of all time. I didn't dare demand a better explanation, though. Partly because I was afraid the cop would hear, and partly because I kind of genuinely *didn't* want to find out.

The cop strolled casually down the platform, looking around with practiced detachment. To all the world, he probably looked like he was doing a routine check for, I don't know, drug dealers or something. But I knew he was looking for us. I held my breath and pressed my body against the controller box as hard as I could.

He paused when he got close to us, looking around with narrowed eyes. He sniffed the air, and for a second I thought I could see the movement of antennae superimposed behind the façade of his human face.

"Little girls," he said in a singsong voice. Goosebumps rippled across my skin at the sound. "Come out, come out, wherever you are."

I glanced over at Shailene. Her scowl was gone. Now she looked almost as nervous as I felt.

He sniffed the air again, then started to move forward, disappearing from view behind one of the massive concrete columns supporting the roof of the platform. I exhaled, but Shailene put her arm in front of me, making me freeze in place. "Don't move," she breathed.

"But my train...!" I whispered in protest. It would be rolling in any second now. If I wanted to get away from this craziness, that would be my last chance for another half an hour.

Shailene looked like she was about to say something snide, but then her eyes widened, and she hissed, "Shh!"

I looked up in alarm. The officer was approaching us again, this time on our side of the guardrail. He sniffed the air once more, eyeing the controller box warily. "You can't hide from me, girls," he said, his voice gravelly. "I know you're here."

Shailene's eyebrows were drawn. She'd shifted her weight onto the balls of her feet. In her right hand was a stun gun. She was going to rush him. My heart pounded in my ears.

The officer took a step closer, looking around, his eyes wandering just over our heads.

Shailene flicked the safety switch on the stun gun. It made a soft click.

In an instant, the officer was on her, grabbing her around the throat with hands that flickered, shimmering into claws and then back again. The stun gun fell from her hand, skittering across the ground and disappearing over the side of the platform. I gasped, frozen in place.

"Too slow, Striker," the officer—creature—hissed in her face. "Now you need to come with me. Your friends are waiting for you."

"Where are they?" Shailene choked.

The officer tightened his grip. "You'll find out soon enough."

He didn't even look at me. Now was my chance to get the hell out of there. But I couldn't just leave Shailene with that *thing*. I didn't know her from a load of hay, but I wasn't an asshole. I had to do something. If only she hadn't lost that stun gun! Electricity seemed to incapacitate them...

The ground rumbled beneath us—my train was pulling into the station. I just had a few seconds. Before I could think twice, I lunged to my feet, tackling the officer as hard as I could.

He teetered for a moment on the edge of the platform before tumbling down onto the tracks. He screamed as his body connected with the electrified third rail, the last of his human façade fading away. The creature looked at me for an instant through prismatic, insect-like eyes, his pointed mandibles quivering.

"You," he said. Though his words didn't quite seem to be English, I still understood them. "Why—?"

Before he could finish his sentence, the train came thundering into the station, crushing the creature like a bug on a car windshield. Wind and monster-guts pelted me as I stood there staring, numb and shaking.

"Laura," I heard Shailene say from behind me. I turned to face her, a grin starting to form on my lips, but was met with a glower in response. "Why did you do that?" she demanded.

My jaw dropped. "Um, because he was strangling you?"

"I had it under control," she snapped, though her red face showed that she knew it was a lie. "Now how am I supposed to find out what they did with Leah and Joanie?"

I just stared at her, my mouth moving wordlessly. She picked up my overnight bag and tossed it at me—hard. I caught it with a grunt of surprise.

"Just get out of here," she said.

"Are you kidding me?" I sputtered. "I just saved your life from some kind of bug monster, and I don't even get a thank you?"

"Thanks *so* much," she said, her voice dripping sarcasm. "Now I think you have a train to catch. Wouldn't want you to miss it."

I gaped at her a moment longer, anger boiling in the pit of my stomach. Then I turned and stormed onto the train, slamming my bag onto the floor just as the pneumatic doors swished closed.

I looked out the window as the train started to move.

Shailene was already gone. But just as the platform disappeared from view, I saw him standing there. It was just for an instant, but I could have sworn he was staring back at me. A shiver ran down my spine.

The man in the black trenchcoat.

- Chapter 3 -

My head was in a complete fog by the time I made it back to the Gam-Lam house. I felt like I was sleepwalking.

It didn't help matters that the house was almost completely deserted, since most of the girls were either home for spring break or partying it up in Florida somewhere. The brightly-lit halls of the big brick house (poor planning, really, in an earthquake-prone city like ours) were eerily quiet, adding to the dreamlike effect. I tossed my overnight bag onto my bed in the large room I shared with the other freshman girls, and then followed the sound of TV speakers into the second-floor lounge down the hall.

My big, Ana, was sprawled across the black leather sectional watching the five o'clock news. She looked up from the bowl of sugary cereal she'd been shoveling into her mouth and grinned. "Laura," she said around a mouthful of marshmallows. "There you are! I was starting to get worried. Weren't you supposed to be back here hours ago?"

I shrugged. "Got held up in Everett." Which, of course, was a total lie. What I'd actually been doing—since leaving the San Luis station, anyway—was staring off into space questioning my sanity. When my train had gotten to the St. Francis stop, I'd just sat there. I'd continued to sit there for the next dozen stops, until the train was gliding past the blue waters of the Bay, and I could see the spires of Bayview University. I'd never seen their campus before. It honestly didn't look all that different from St. Francis, though of course I could never say that in front of any of my Mariner friends without getting burned at the stake for heresy.

Finally, after racking up enough stops that this month's PeRT bill was sure to make my mother erupt like Krakatau, I'd gotten back over to City East and headed home. But in that time, I had come to a decision: I wasn't going to tell anyone what had happened that day. I didn't like being that person who *kept secrets*, but no matter how I looked at it, there was just no way that I could explain it that wouldn't make me sound—at best—drunk out of my mind.

And, besides, Shailene had made it abundantly clear that she didn't want any more of my help. So the best thing was to just forget it entirely and get back to my normal life. It didn't involve me, anyway.

Ana swallowed and set the empty cereal bowl on the coffee table with a clatter. "So, how was the wedding?"

I rolled my eyes. "Every bit as fun as you'd expect." I started to tell her all about what had happened with Lola while the newscaster droned about the latest poll numbers for the upcoming election. But I broke off mid-sentence when I heard him say, "And now for local news. Two Bayview University cheerleaders were reported missing earlier today..."

I jerked my head over to the screen just as the picture switched to a live reporter standing in some kind of large gymnasium. In the background, I could see girls milling around wearing cheer uniforms I didn't recognize. The text at the bottom of the screen said that it was the Regional College Cheerleader and Dance Team Championships.

"That's right, Jerry," the reporter said, "Leah Martin and Joanie Fitzgerald were reported missing earlier today when they failed to appear at the regional cheer meet here at the Jones Athletics Center. Neither girl has been heard from by friends or family since two days ago, but it's believed they may be traveling eastbound toward the town of Everett."

Gee, I wonder where they got that idea. I narrowed my eyes. Somehow I got the feeling that they'd been heard from more recently than two days ago—by the other cheerleaders at least. Did they lie to get the police involved sooner?

Then the camera zoomed out, and my breath caught in my throat as a petite girl with braids I definitely recognized came into view. "I'm here with Erikka Johnson, one of the missing girls' squadmates," said the reporter.

Erikka nodded, her eyes watery. "We're just so worried about them. Leah's our captain—we weren't even able to perform at the meet without them. I don't know what could have happened to them. They're such nice, normal girls."

The snort came out before I could stop it. Ana looked at me in surprise. "What's that about?" she asked, her eyebrow up. "Do you know them or something?"

"No, not really," I said quickly. "It's just, I mean. Cheerleaders. From Bayview. I'm sure they decided to blow off that stupid meet and hit the beach in Cabo or something." I could feel Ana's dark eyes staring at me, but I kept my burning face riveted on the TV screen, hoping she wouldn't press. A second later, I wished I hadn't—because the camera moved slightly, and I saw that standing next to

Erikka was Shailene, looking flawless and elegant, her mouth pulled into a dainty pout of concern. No sign of the bug guts that I'd been picking out of my own hair all afternoon, or the scowl I'd last seen on her face. My cheeks grew even hotter against my will. It didn't matter that she was pretty, I scolded myself. She was still a bitch.

I jumped to my feet. "Well, can't sit around watching TV all day. That English paper isn't going to write itself."

Ana looked at me oddly. "Laura, you sure you're okay?"

I laughed. "Oh, yeah, I'm fine. I'm just tired. You know how big family events can be." I knew she did. Ana had an enormous Mexican family; she and I had bonded over it when I rushed, and that was part of the reason she'd been eager to take me as her little. We got each other on a spiritual level.

She pursed her lips. "Okay, well... Don't forget, we don't have kitchen service this week. Do you want to go get some dinner later?"

"No, I think I'll just have some toast or something. Rest my stomach after all that lumpia." I smiled tightly, and she gave me a thin laugh in return. She still looked worried. It made me feel even worse about lying, but I couldn't tell her how I really knew those cheerleaders. Even thinking it sounded ridiculous.

It doesn't matter, I told myself, heading back down the

hall to my room. I just needed to put it behind me. In a few days, I'd have forgotten about it, and everything would go back to normal.

I TOLD MYSELF THAT, but then what did I do as soon as I got to my room? Got right on the internet and started Googling everything I could find.

I started with "Bayview University cheerleaders." The top results were news stories about the two missing girls— "missing" for two days, all the news sites kept reminding me, even though I'd seen them less than six hours ago.

Below the news articles was a link to the Swordsmen Athletics website, which had a roster of the cheer squad with each of the members' pictures. That must be where all the news channels had gotten their pictures of Leah and Joanie, the other girl from the train who had looked at me with those pale green eyes before disappearing from view. I scrolled quickly down the page, but there was no information apart from the squad members' names, projected graduation years and photos. I refused to let my eyes linger on Shailene Peterson, freshman. Not any longer than it took to register her name, anyway. It still seemed familiar to me, but I couldn't quite place it. Thinking about it was starting to give me a headache.

I browsed through a few more pages of results, but there was nothing of interest. Bayview's cheer squad was small, but it had a reputation for being elite among those who cared about that sort of thing. They'd won the regional championships the last three years in a row—I couldn't help snickering to myself, remembering how Erikka said on the news that they'd had to forfeit this year due to the missing teammates—and several national championships as well. The squad was known for its "almost superhuman athleticism and agility" (that's what popped up when I searched "Bayview cheerleaders superhuman"). But there was no information about them being, you know, monster hunters or whatever they were, so the cheerleader angle seemed to be a bust.

The next thing I tried was that weird word Shailene had mentioned: "Anesidoran." I had to try a few different spellings, but finally I got it. Anesidora: an alternate name for Pandora, the one with the box (or, more correctly, *jar*— as Wikipedia so kindly informed me) from Greek mythology.

I frowned. Pandora was supposed to have unleashed evil monsters into the world. If those bug creatures in cops' clothing didn't count as evil monsters, I didn't know what would.

I scrolled through a few pages of increasingly random nonsense, each seeming to have less and less to do with what I was looking for. Finally, I clicked away from a page about alien abductions near Area 51 and closed my eyes, massaging my stiff jaw with my fingers. My headache was worse than ever. It was starting to remind me of how my Auntie Cristina described migraines, though I'd never had one myself. I needed to just forget this and start working on my English paper before this headache took me entirely out of commission.

Just one more search. Just to satisfy my curiosity.

Before I could talk myself out of it, my fingers were flying across my laptop's keyboard, typing the one phrase I'd been most itching to search all night but hadn't had the nerve to.

"Shailene Peterson, Everett Middle School."

I pressed *enter*, and the dull throbbing behind my eyes suddenly turned into a sharp stabbing pain. It hurt to keep my eyes open, but closing them didn't seem to help, either. Sucking my breath in through clenched teeth, I hunched forward, pressing my head between my hands to try to abate the pain. My ears started to ring, the sound growing louder and louder until I just couldn't take it anymore.

Everything went black.

SOMEONE WAS WATCHING ME.

Even though my eyes were closed, I knew someone was there, staring at me. It startled me awake, and I tried to fling my eyelids open, but they were heavy and wouldn't move. My vision swam with colors. I wanted to see, but I couldn't.

"Laura."

At last I managed to pry my eyes open and immediately wished I hadn't. Because there was Mr. Trenchcoat standing over me, his skin oscillating all the colors that had been swimming in front of me just a minute ago.

I screamed.

"Laura!"

I blinked and the man in the trenchcoat was gone. In his place was Ana. She hurried over to my side and perched at the foot of the bed, looking at me fretfully. "Are you okay?"

I glanced around the room in confusion. "How did I get here?" I asked. I was somehow in my bed, but I couldn't remember moving from my desk.

Ana leaned over and handed me a glass of orange juice that had been sitting on the nightstand next to me. "I think you're sick. You fell asleep at your desk or something, and when I stuck my head in here a couple hours ago you started going, 'My head hurts, my head hurts.' So I helped you get into bed."

I pulled my knees into my chest. "I don't remember," I said. "Sorry."

"Don't apologize!" She smiled. "I think you had a fever. Did the aspirin help? You took some before you went to sleep."

I nodded. "It must have. I don't have a headache anymore at least."

"Good." She hesitated. "And listen. If you want to talk, remember I'm here, yeah?" I quirked my eyebrow, confused, and she laughed embarrassedly. "On your computer. That girl you were Facebook stalking, Shailene?" She patted my foot as I continued to stare blankly at her. "I recognized her from the TV earlier, when you got all pissy. She's your ex, right?"

My jaw dropped. "Uh, no," I said. I didn't even remember pulling up her Facebook page. All I remembered was clicking *search* on Google and then my head exploding.

"Oh, sorry. But you know her, right? It said on her page that she's from Everett. I closed it for you, though, so you wouldn't get upset again."

I smiled tightly, my mind a blur. "Thanks," was all I

could manage to say. Why didn't I remember any of this?

"Well, let me know if you want to talk," Ana said, taking my empty orange juice glass from me. "Try not to think about her, and get some sleep. The Deltas are going to breakfast at Gunther's in the morning. If you're feeling okay, do you want to come?" The Deltas were Ana's pledge class, mostly girls two years ahead of me. Most of them had stayed at the house over spring break, though I hadn't seen them when I'd gotten back.

"Sure," I said. Ana nodded and patted my foot again, and despite my grogginess from the dream, I felt that familiar rush of affection that I'd experienced so often in the months since Big Reveal and initiation—the feeling that I was the luckiest little in the world. Ana was more than just some girl who'd been assigned to me at random. She was like the sister I'd never had. All the cousins and uncles and aunties were nothing like having a real sibling. But joining Gam-Lam? It gave me what I'd been missing.

After Ana left, I looked around the big room at the rows of empty beds. I didn't know how I was supposed to sleep alone in here, not if I was going to have nightmares about the Technicolor Dude in a Trenchcoat staring at me all night.

I stood up and moved to look out the window, down at our small garden. Fog had rolled in from the Bay, obscuring the tops of the trees and coating the wrought iron bench in the courtyard with moisture. Little dewdrops trickled off the house's letters, *Gamma Sigma Lambda.*

Shailene is from Everett, I thought, running my finger across the glass. *So she's probably the girl I remember from middle school.* But why didn't I remember more about her? I supposed it could have been just one of those things—it *was* six years ago, after all, and if I hadn't known her that well then I probably *wouldn't* remember much. But it felt wrong somehow, especially after today.

Why did thinking about it make my head hurt so much?

I resolved not to think about it for probably the eight-hundredth time. Then I pulled the blinds shut and went to bed.

- Chapter 4 -

If you really want to get your mind off something, I recommend one of Gunther's Dutch babies. Seriously, just try to stay stressed with a light, fluffy popover the size of a bicycle tire—drizzled in lemon and coated with powdered sugar—in front of you. It's a physical impossibility.

Beside me, Makeisha, one of the Deltas I'd gone to breakfast with, laughed. "My favorite part of coming here is seeing the look on Laura's face when they bring one of those things out. It's like she's having a religious experience," she said, elbowing me playfully.

"I can't help it if I love food," I replied solemnly, though a grin was threatening to break through. "It's part of my heritage."

She quirked her eyebrows. "Including German pancakes?"

"That's from my dad's side."

Everyone laughed, and across the table, my big caught my eye. I could tell she was relieved to see me feeling better. And, honestly, I did. A good night's sleep had put some distance between me and the events of the day before. In a few weeks, I was sure, I'd forget the whole thing.

Just like I'd apparently forgotten Shailene.

Breakfast went swimmingly until the end, when we got up as a group to pay the cashier and noticed the TV over the register. The news was playing another story about the Bayview cheerleaders.

"That's so scary," Natalia, a senior, said. "Do you think it was a kidnapping? My cousin goes to Bayview, and he said that's what everyone's saying. What if it's some kind of fetishist with a thing for cheerleaders?"

I chuckled shakily, pulling my card out of my wallet. "Well, as long as he sticks with them and doesn't switch to sorority girls, I guess we're safe."

We headed out of the restaurant and started back toward the Gam-Lam house. Gunther's was just a few blocks away from campus, but going back was uphill all the way.

"Time to work off those sausages," Makeisha said, smacking her stomach and laughing as we started up the incline. It was early enough—and cold enough—that the fog that had rolled in last night still hadn't burned off yet. The businesses around us were shrouded in mist, the signs over their doors smudgy and barely legible. Other St. Francis students, starting to trickle back today for one last weekend of partying before school resumed on Monday, milled around us in groups.

I felt oddly unsettled. It was probably just because of what Natalia had said, but I felt like I was being watched. I kept thinking I saw shadows out of the corner of my eye, things moving too fast to be human.

"Probably just birds," I muttered under my breath.

"What'd you say, *mija?*" Ana said, glancing over her shoulder at me.

"This hill is killing me," I replied without missing a beat. "Aren't you supposed to wait twenty minutes after you eat before exercising?"

A shadow moved to my right, and a streak of red shot past me, fog swirling around her figure. That definitely wasn't a bird. And it wasn't my imagination, either. I stopped dead in my tracks.

"You okay, Laura?" Natalia asked.

Thinking quickly, I started rummaging through my

purse. I couldn't let her get away. "Crap," I said. "I think I left my wallet at Gunther's."

"Are you sure?" asked Ana.

"Yeah. It's not in here. Now that I think of it, I remember setting it on the counter in front of the register." I shoved my purse back up onto my shoulder. "I'm just going to run back and get it."

"You want us to come with you?" Makeisha said.

"No, no, it's fine," I replied, edging away from the group. "I'll just be a minute. You guys go on ahead." I turned and hurried back down the hill before any of them could protest further. But I didn't stop when I reached Gunther's; after all, my wallet was safely in my purse. Instead, I kept running all the way down to the corner, following the red blur that—I swear—looked like one of the Bayview cheerleaders on one of those old Razor scooters. What next, a pair of rollerblades?

At the corner, I lost sight of the girl. I paused, wondering if I'd been mistaken. But no—I knew what I'd seen. Seconds later, I heard a crash and raised voices. I darted forward, following the sound to a service alley that ran behind Gunther's. I was just steps away when the sky above my head lit up with bright red lightning, eerily diffused by the fog. There was a scream, and then a crash of thunder followed, rattling the windows of the buildings around me. I let out a cry and ducked, covering my ears. Then it was quiet.

Across the street, a guy who had been selling hemp jewelry on the corner lifted up his sunglasses (*Seriously, on a foggy day like this?*) and stared at me with his mouth open. I gave him the dirtiest look I could muster and rushed into the alley.

It was empty.

I crept forward slowly, looking around at the bedlam. A trash can near the service entrance to Gunther's had tipped over, its contents strewn all over the wet asphalt. The air smelled like something burning, but the alley was eerily quiet. It was like no one had been here at all. But I knew I'd seen her. And there was that red lightning...

There was a soft rustle behind me. I whirled around. Standing at the entrance to the alley, boxing me in, was Shailene. She was wearing black yoga pants and a red letterman jacket zipped up all the way to her neck to protect against the chill damp air. Her dark, sideswept hair fell loosely around her shoulders like a curtain, framing her stony face. She breathed heavily, puffs of mist rising from her mouth in bursts.

"What are you doing here?" I asked as soon as I found my voice.

"I should be asking you that. Where's Leslie?"

"Leslie?" I repeated. "The girl on the scooter?" Shailene nodded. "I don't know. I saw her come in here, but there was this loud noise, and the sky got all red, and—"

A noise that didn't quite sound human tore from Shailene's throat. She abruptly turned and kicked the dumpster beside her with an enormous crash, making me jump. She squeezed her eyes shut, and for a second I thought she was going to cry. I started to move forward, hesitantly, reaching for her shoulder, but then I pulled back. It felt like I was intruding.

"Three in two days," she murmured, barely audible. Then she opened her eyes and the sorrow was gone, replaced with cold fury. "Okay, who the hell are you?" she demanded.

I took a step backward. "I-I don't—"

"Don't give me that crap. Every time you turn up, our girls start vanishing."

"That doesn't have anything to do with me!" I protested.

"Oh, really? Then how come there were sentries following you just now? Leslie was trying to lure them away from you, but then you broke away from your group. And now she's gone." She crossed her arms, glaring at me.

"Sentries don't waste their time with ordinary humans. They leave that to the technicians. Sentries are only interested in *us*. But you can't be one of us. HQ has a record of all the free lab rats in the state. But no record of you." She'd started advancing on me as she spoke. I backed up until I hit the cold metal of the dumpster behind me. "You're supposed to just be a normal human, yet you see and hear everything. So who the hell are you?"

Her face was just inches from mine. My heart pounded in my throat. I wish I could say it was because I was afraid, like any normal person would be in this situation. I knew I should be; but at this close proximity, something else was coming over me. And it wasn't even hormones, either. That weird déjà vu feeling was back, overpoweringly. Like she and I had been in this position before—only she hadn't wanted to wring my neck back then. Quite the opposite, in fact. The memory teased at the sides of my mind, but it was blurry and muted. My temples started to throb.

I turned my face away from hers, focusing on the dingy alley instead. "I don't know why they're following me. I really am nobody. I'm just Laura Clark, like I told you yesterday. I don't know why I can see these things. I didn't ask for any of this. So please, just—" My voice broke off. I wanted to say *go away*, but the words wouldn't come out. I tried, but my mouth just couldn't form them. What the hell was wrong with my body? The headache was returning with a vengeance, along with nauseating tunnel vision.

"Laura?"

Startled, I glanced at Shailene. She looked a little green around the gills herself. Her eyes were out of focus, staring at me but not seeing me. She murmured something—possibly my name again—but I couldn't hear it over the ringing in my ears.

Then a woman's voice, bold and clear, echoed across the alleyway. "Striker Peterson."

Shailene jolted, her eyes clearing, and she turned. When she moved away from me, the tunnel vision abruptly receded. I took a shaky breath and looked at the newcomer. She was a tall, muscular blond woman, her hair pulled back in a slick ponytail.

"Coach," Shailene said.

The woman folded her arms across her chest. "Stand down."

"But, Coach," Shailene protested, "now Leslie's gone. I can't sense her anywhere. And she's the last person who saw her."

"I *said*, stand down," the woman repeated.

When Shailene moved away from me, the blonde stepped forward to shake my hand. Bewildered, I let her.

"Pleasure to meet you, Laura Clark," she said in a silky smooth voice.

I felt like I'd been transported to *The Twilight Zone*. "Uh, thanks," I said. "Who are you? And how do you know my name?"

She opened the lapel of her jacket and pulled out an extremely official-looking badge. "Special agent Janice Sheldon. I'm with the I.G.A., and I'm going to need you to come with me."

- Chapter 5 -

"Wait a second," I said dubiously, peering through the tinted windshield of the SUV at the tall white-stone campanile looming over us. "You said you're with the I.G.A. So why did you bring me here?"

Janice Sheldon smiled over at me from the driver's seat. "Don't worry. You'll understand everything once we get to my office."

I frowned. "No offense, but that sounds pretty shady. Shouldn't I have my lawyer with me or something?" Not that I *had* a lawyer, of course. I suppose there was always my uncle Julian who lived in New York, but he was a divorce attorney, and he wasn't even licensed in this state. I didn't know how much use he would be in a case like this.

"You're not under arrest, Laura," Janice said with a

laugh. "And I think you'll agree that the things that have been happening to you are already pretty shady. I just want to help you understand what's going on a little better."

I slumped back against the leather seat and nodded. Considering their previous modes of transportation, I had half expected this Janice Sheldon to haul me off to the local I.G.A. branch on a tandem bike. But no—she'd had a snazzy black SUV parked in a garage a few blocks away. It was relatively nondescript apart from those orange license plates that state vehicles have, the ones with no registration sticker. I guessed the I.G.A. probably didn't need to pay a fee to the DMV like the rest of us schlubs.

She'd ushered me, smoothly but firmly, into the front seat of the vehicle. Shailene hadn't come with us. "Reconnoiter with the others," I'd heard Janice tell her before she closed my passenger door. "Start tracking. See if you can find signs of the other sentries."

"What about Leslie?" Shailene had asked.

"We'll find her. But don't be distracted. Stick to tracking the sentries."

Shailene had glared at me through the windshield for an instant, and I'd glared back. Then she'd nodded curtly, turning on her heel and disappearing back toward the street. Janice had gotten in the car, and that had been that. She hadn't said much on the drive over here. But the place she'd taken me to was the last place I'd expected. Although, considering my luck these last two days, I really shouldn't have been surprised.

Bayview University.

Janice pulled the SUV into a spot in the faculty parking lot behind the gym, and I remembered with a jolt that Shailene had called her *coach*. Was this Bayview's cheer coach, then? Did I.G.A. agents usually take side jobs like that? It might explain a few things about the weird behavior of the cheerleaders around here. The I.G.A. was a government agency like the F.B.I. The International and Global Affairs bureau—I remembered vaguely that my dad had worked for them as a contractor when he'd first gotten out of college, way before I'd been born. They usually dealt with terrorist threats. Was some terrorist group making genetically engineered monsters or something? What, bombs weren't good enough anymore?

As Janice got out of the car, I quickly slid my phone out of my purse. Fingers flying, I texted, *Hey dad, did you ever know anyone named Janice Sheldon in Nevada?*

I'd just pressed *send* on that when Janice opened my door for me. I wasn't quick enough; she caught the movement of my hand tossing my phone back into my purse. "Ah, I'm afraid I'm going to need to take that," she said, holding her hand out.

I blanched. "Seriously? I just wanted to let my roommate know I wouldn't be back for a few hours."

She smiled, one of those fake cheerleader smiles that I couldn't imagine ever crossing Shailene's face. "Sorry. It's policy. You can have it back when the meeting is over."

Reluctantly, I handed my phone over to her. Janice slid it into her jacket pocket and closed the car door for me. She guided me across the parking lot toward the athletics building. It was painted a deep red color, with the word *Swordsmen* scrawled in enormous letters along the wall under the high, domed roof. A silver-and-gold pirate's cutlass pierced through the cursive letters.

"Right this way," she said, leading me across the empty gym. Our shoes squeaked on the waxed wood floors, the sound echoing up to the ceiling. I followed her through a door and scoffed.

"The women's locker room? Are you kidding me?"

She leveled her gaze at me and my jaw snapped shut. She flicked a switch next to the door, illuminating rows of red metal lockers. In between them and the shower stalls on the back wall was another door with a window in the center covered with dark brown blinds. "My office is in here," she said, opening the door.

I followed her into the small room, which was barely big enough to hold one shabby desk. The wall over the desk was lined with plaques and certificates showcasing the Swordsmen cheerleaders' accolades over the last several years. A framed photo in the center showed Janice with the squad from last year, holding up the regional championship trophy. Shailene was nowhere to be seen. *Of course not,* I thought. *She's a freshman, like me.*

"I thought you said you were an I.G.A. agent," I said, trying to keep the sarcasm out of my voice. "This looks like a P.E. teacher's office."

Janice sighed wearily, closing the door behind me. "You certainly are impatient." She pulled a lanyard out from under her shirt. A key card swung from the end. Holding the card in one hand, she nudged the photo to the side. Beneath it, a small panel was embedded in the wall. She swiped her card, then pressed her thumb onto the digital display next to the slot. Before I could blink, the floor opened up, the desk dropped smoothly out of view, and a doorway opened in the wall.

My jaw dropped. "What the hell is this, *Get Smart?*" was all I could manage.

Janice rolled her eyes. "Just come on, Laura."

I followed her through the door into a small, unfurnished room. The wall slid shut behind us, and then the floor lurched. I gasped, bracing myself against the wall. It was only then that I realized that the room was an elevator. We were moving, but I couldn't tell if it was up or down. After a few moments, I decided it must be down—the trip was taking too long for a building that was only two or three stories tall at the most.

Then the elevator shuddered to a stop, and the wall slid open again. My eyes widened.

We definitely weren't in the gym anymore.

"Where are we?" I whispered.

Janice smirked. "Welcome to the I.G.A."

It was an enormous space, almost like a warehouse. And it was pandemonium. There were dozens—if not hundreds—of people here. Rows of desks were lined with computer monitors, some people seated in front of them working in silence, others with groups of two or three talking quietly amongst one another, looking over each other's shoulders. It looked like the bridge of the Helicarrier, or mission control at NASA, or something. On the concrete wall in front of me was the familiar emblem of the I.G.A., a stylized globe overlaid with the organization's letters in vaguely-1970s-looking text. My eyes slid over it unseeingly as I stared around at all the people here; then I blinked and jerked my gaze back at it, not sure if I'd read right. *I.G.A.*—I knew it was supposed to stand for *International and Global Affairs*. But that's not what this sign said. There on the wall in solid gold (well, gold-colored, anyway) letters it read, plain as day: *Inter-Galactic Affairs.*

Excuse me, *what?*

Janice Sheldon was still smirking at me. "Speechless for once, I see."

I glared at her. "As if. What is this place, really? This can't be the I.G.A. I've seen their building downtown. It's across the street from City Hall."

"Ah, she is civic-minded," Janice said, leading me between the rows of desks. I pursed my lips. I certainly wasn't going to tell her that I'd only been down that way one time, when I'd gotten lost looking for the opera house. I'd never been down that way before, but the Gam-Lams were all going to see Makeisha's sister in *The Nutcracker.* "That's our public office. This is our true hub of operations."

I gave her a look as she stopped at one of the computer stations. "Under the Bayview University gym?"

The computer monitor lit up, prompting Janice for a password. She typed something in quickly, then leaned close to a webcam mounted on the top of the monitor. "*Retinal scan match. System boot,*" the computer said.

"Bayview University is administered by the I.G.A.," Janice said once the computer had finished. "Our facility runs under the entire campus."

I blinked once, twice. "*What?* Why? I've heard of state schools, but this is a little ridiculous, isn't it? I mean, what the heck would the I.G.A. want a college for?"

"This is why." She gestured to the computer screen. I moved forward, peering over her shoulder.

"'Abductee Rehabilitation Program'," I read. Under the bold header, rows of photos filled the screen, like a high school yearbook. Dozens of faces of people my age, maybe a little younger, maybe a little older. "Abductees? Like kidnapping victims?"

"Of a sort." Janice watched me, folding her arms and leaning against the desk as I scrolled down the page, trying to take in all the photos. "Anesidorans tend to favor adolescents for their experiments. Their bodies haven't finished forming yet, so they take better to the modifications and implants."

I stopped scrolling, my finger frozen on the mouse. Anesidorans—those bug things from the train station. *Inter-Galactic Affairs.* Did she seriously mean—?

"Aliens?" I said, my voice barely more than a squeak. "Alien abductions?"

Janice nodded once, slowly. "Now you're catching on."

I spluttered incomprehensibly. "You're trying to tell me that all the kids at Bayview University are alien abductees?"

"Not all of them. Some are relatives of abductees. These experiments have been going on for the past hundred years or so since the invasion from Nibiru began. They modify the victims' actual DNA. That means the physiological alterations are often passed down to the children and even grandchildren of abductees. Those kids need a support system, a way of learning to control their abilities."

"The Xavier Institute for Gifted Alien Lab Rats?" I said.

Janice chuckled, and for the first time it seemed like she was laughing with me, not at me. I smiled back and turned away from the computer, trying to process this information.

"Okay, so you're telling me that those things I saw at the train station were aliens. From—'Nibiru'?" That word sounded familiar to me, but I couldn't quite place why.

Janice nodded and gestured to a map on her desk. It looked like a chart of the solar system, but there was something abnormal about it. It took me a minute to notice what was amiss—there was an extra planet, way past Pluto. It was enormous, bigger than Jupiter. They definitely hadn't mentioned that thing in high school physics.

"That's Nibiru," Janice said, gesturing to the circle on the map. "Also known as Planet X."

"Okay, now I know you're full of it," I said. "Seriously? *Planet X?* Star of 1950s B-movies? That thing that all the crazy guys in the tinfoil hats are warning us about?" I realized that was where I'd heard the word *Nibiru* before. There was a billboard off the interstate that had been a particular favorite of mine as a kid, urging us that Planet X was on a collision course with Earth, and that if we didn't repent by a certain date, we would all be doomed to eternal damnation. The billboard had been there for years, unchanged in every way except that the date of our supposed impending annihilation kept getting moved further into the future—conveniently, every time the previous doomsday passed.

Janice shrugged. "Would it be cliché to say that all the legends are true?"

I closed my eyes for a long moment, breathing in. "Okay. I'll bite. So we're being invaded by aliens from Planet X. And they're abducting our teenagers for... what, exactly?"

Her expression grew serious. "They're building an army. One that can destroy us from the inside out. They're monsters, Laura. Pandora's Box. It's what they do." She crossed her arms. "Every year, Anesidorans kidnap hundreds of children from all over the world. They don't give them back willingly. The I.G.A.'s special operations unit rescues the kids we can, but it's a tiny fraction of the total that are taken."

I opened my mouth, but no sound came. It was impossible. But I had seen the proof with my own eyes.

"So the Bayview cheer squad?" I finally managed.

"They are our next generation of special operations agents. Our elite team."

"And someone is targeting them?"

She nodded.

"But what does that have to do with me? I wasn't abducted. I'm pretty sure I would remember if I was."

"But you can see Anesidorans in their true forms," Janice said. "Ordinary humans don't have that ability. And Shailene says you saw our girls yesterday on the train, even though they would have been cloaked."

I frowned. "So what does that mean? Someone in my family was an abductee?"

"I did a search on your name and I couldn't find any indication of it. But based on your capabilities, I would say almost certainly—"

I only half heard her. My mind had suddenly fixed on my father—my boring, unassuming, white-bread dad—who had spent two years working for the I.G.A. in Nevada before dropping everything to move to Everett with my mom when they got married. Could he...?

Janice was saying, "We have a series of aptitude tests that I'd like to have you take, if you're willing, that would measure—"

"Wait, hold that thought," I said, lifting my hands, trying to process this all. "I have an idea, but—"

I was interrupted by the blaring sound of a klaxon. I flinched, throwing my hands over my ears. My first instinct was to dive under the nearest desk in case this was an earthquake alarm, but next to me, Janice merely unzipped her jacket, revealing a shoulder holster, and pulled out a handgun.

"What's happening?" I asked, shouting to hear myself over the alarm. Around us, pandemonium raged as agents jumped up from their work stations, some trying to quickly shut down their computers, others drawing weapons like Janice.

"Unauthorized entry," Janice said, looking to the elevator we'd come into the facility through. The elevator doors shuddered open. I ducked behind Janice as she lifted her gun.

My dad burst into the room.

"Dad!" I gasped at the same time Janice lowered her gun and said, "Gregg."

I looked between them in confusion. My dad's name was Phil, not Greg. But the look of immediate recognition confirmed the suspicion I'd had since Janice brought me here: my dad definitely knew a Janice Sheldon from the I.G.A.

"Stand down," Janice called, and the agents around the facility hesitantly lowered their weapons. I scooted between my dad and Janice just in case, though, since the look on her face could only be described as *murderous.* "Now things are starting to make sense," she muttered.

"Maybe to you two, but not to me. Dad, what are you doing here?" I asked.

He stepped forward, brushing past me and shoving me (I suppose you could say protectively, though that didn't make me any less annoyed) behind him. "No," he said, "the real question is, what is my *daughter* doing here? My dispensation specifically indicates that the I.G.A. was not to contact me or my family after my discharge."

Janice glared back at him. "Your daughter has involved herself with I.G.A. affairs."

He looked at me in alarm. "Laura?"

I shrugged helplessly. I was beyond lost at this point.

He turned back to Janice. "I'll see to it that she doesn't get in your way again." He put his arm around my shoulder, guiding me back toward the elevator.

"Excuse me?" I said, ducking out from under his arm.

My biggest pet peeve was my dad steering me around like he had when I'd been a toddler. He had no concept of personal space. "Would someone mind explaining what's going on here?"

"They're targeting her, Gregg," Janice said. My dad froze midstep, half glancing at her over his shoulder. "There's no way you can protect her on her own. All you're doing by keeping her from us is putting her at risk."

He set his jaw. "I'll be the judge of that." He pushed me into the elevator, and the doors slid shut behind us.

"Excuse me?" I whirled on my dad. "Would you mind explaining what the hell just happened?"

"You texted me, remember?" He folded his arms, seeming miffed that I wasn't thanking him profusely for coming to my rescue.

"Yeah, I texted you, but a simple text back would have sufficed. I wasn't expecting you to come bursting in here like a psycho. And how did you get down here so fast?"

"I was in the area." I gave him an incredulous look, but he ignored me. "Janice Sheldon is bad news, Laura. The whole I.G.A. is. I don't want them coming around you."

"It wasn't exactly their fault, Dad. Something weird is going on with me. There are these weird bug things—"

"Sentries."

"Yeah, those. Wait. So you do know! Does that mean you..." I trailed off, unsure what to say. I was having one of those weird out-of-body moments where you hear yourself as someone else would hear you, and realize you sound like a complete lunatic. "Were you an abductee?"

"No."

"You're lying."

He closed his eyes and pinched the bridge of his nose. "I'm not getting into this with you, Laura. I can honestly tell you that I was not an abductee. I can also honestly tell you that, regardless of what you might have been told just now, the I.G.A. are not your friends. What have I always said? The most dangerous words in the English language are, 'I'm from the government and I'm here to help.'"

I scowled. "Somehow I always got the feeling that was more about the Internal Revenue Service than about an invasion from outer space."

The elevator doors opened back out onto Janice Sheldon's office. Dad steered me out of this and back into the fortunately-still-empty girls' locker room, which I realized was a really creepy place to put an apparently co-ed entrance to a secret government facility. I wondered if there was also an entrance in the boys' room.

"Come on, Dad, this is ridiculous," I snapped as we

made our way back out into the main gym. "I'm an adult. Stop treating me like a kid. You don't want me going around the I.G.A.? Fine. Give me a better reason than just 'I said so.'"

"I can't."

I made a noise of exasperation from the back of my throat. "Then why am I supposed to listen to you? You're not the boss of me." I realized that sounded like an incredibly *not* adult thing to say, considering that I was trying to argue the case that he should start treating me like one. But I couldn't think of a better way to explain it.

"You're right," he said, folding his arms and looking at me seriously. "I'm not the boss of you. You are an adult. But you've lived with me your whole life. Do you trust my judgment?"

I blinked repeatedly. This was an unexpected twist. "I mean, yeah," I said.

"Then I'm asking you, as an adult, to trust me. I'm not able to tell you the whole story. I'm asking you to trust my judgment."

I blinked again. "Okay."

He smiled tightly. "Good. Just forget any of this ever happened. Don't go around these people again. If they keep bothering you, call me."

"But what about those bug things?" I asked.

"Those bug things aren't going to hurt you."

I scoffed. Was he serious? Alien bug creatures were following me all over the Peninsula, and I was supposed to believe that they weren't going to snatch me up and put me on their probulator?

But then again, none of them had actually bothered *me* so far. They'd been *around* me, but when I really thought about it, it was the Bayview cheerleaders they seemed to be after, not me specifically. What was up with that?

My dad opened the gym's side door and held it open for the dark-haired girl just coming in. He stared past her blankly, but she gawked at him, then me. It was Shailene. My face burned, and I looked resolutely down at my feet as she went by. I could feel her trying to meet my gaze, sense her unspoken questions—or demands, knowing her—but with my dad there, she just smiled tightly and headed toward the locker room.

"Oh, and Laura," Dad said, still holding the door open. Out of the corner of my eye, I saw Shailene pause, pretending to tie her shoe so she could listen. I looked up at him, hoping that my face wasn't as red as it felt. "Don't tell your mom about this, okay? She's stressed out enough with all the company. She doesn't need more on her plate right now."

"Sure," I said, brushing past him. He let go of the door, heading blithely toward the parking lot.

I glanced over my shoulder, watching Shailene disappear as the door swung shut.

- Chapter 6 -

Dinner went by in a blur of yelling, the clatter of dishes loaded with prepackaged food, and a generous helping of lies.

The yelling came from the Deltas, who were more than a little bit miffed that I hadn't come back to the house after disappearing to "retrieve my wallet."

"You'd literally *just* finished saying, 'I hope they don't start going after sorority girls,' and then you vanish," Natalia scolded around a mouthful of ramen noodles. "What were we supposed to think?"

The lies, on the other hand, were all me.

"I already told you, I got distracted," I said, peeling back the lid on my container of Easy Mac and turning on the faucet. "I bumped into one of the guys from my public speaking class, and he wanted to practice our presentations for next week." That would have been a much better way to spend the afternoon, honestly. As much as I hated public speaking, anything resembling normality seemed infinitely more appealing than this alternate universe I was living in now.

"You could have answered one of our texts. We were about ready to call the cops," said Makeisha, elbowing her way in front of me to stick her Hot Pocket in the microwave.

I sighed, setting my still-cold and now-soggy macaroni down on the counter to await my turn. I, for one, couldn't wait for kitchen service to start again. This feeding oneself thing was highly overrated. "I lost my phone."

"Losing everything," Natalia groaned, though with all the noodles dripping out of her mouth, it came out more like *"mooshing merving."* She swallowed and clucked her tongue. "Your wallet, your phone... You'd better be careful, chickie, or next up you'll lose your head."

"Sure thing, Mom," I muttered under my breath. The microwave beeped, and I darted forward to yank Makeisha's pizza roll out and shove my macaroni in before anyone else could usurp me. Then I leaned against the small kitchenette counter and folded my arms. "Where's my big at?"

"Date night," Makeisha replied with a waggle of her eyebrows.

My jaw dropped involuntarily. "What? Who with?"

"Some guy from Beta, I think. We had a mixer with them last weekend after you left for Everett."

I tried to keep from making a face. Betas were okay, I guess, as far as fraternity guys go. But I couldn't believe Ana hadn't told me she had a date. We usually told each other everything.

The microwave beeped, and I yanked my mac and cheese out, trudging into the mostly-empty dining room and parking it at one of the long wooden tables. It seemed like the whole damn world had turned upside-down in the last twenty-four hours. I supposed I didn't really have room to complain, considering how evasive I'd been toward Ana last night. But the fact that she'd kept this from me stung worse than I would have expected.

After dinner, I went upstairs to my giant, empty room. It was Friday night, but I didn't feel much like going out after the day—hell, week—I'd had. I opened my laptop up with the intention of working on my English paper, but mostly I just stared at the blank screen and zoned out, listening absently to the noise and squeals of the few girls who were here getting ready for a night on the town.

Around nine o'clock, Natalia stuck her head in the doorway. "Chickie, we're going down to the crawl. Unless you want to come? We could skip the bars and look for a house party if you want."

I smiled tightly. "It's okay. I'm partied out after the wedding."

She winked. "I know the feeling. See you tomorrow."

I tried to concentrate on writing, but my brain felt like it was mired down in quicksand. After an hour passed and I'd only written half a page, I gave up and closed my laptop, standing and stretching. There was too much else on my mind. When I wasn't thinking about the absolute lunacy that had been this afternoon, I was wondering what time Ana was getting home, and whether I should tell her what was going on and risk sounding like a raving maniac, and if this Beta guy she was going out with was good enough for her, and why she hadn't told me about him.

I moved over to the window, resting my forehead against the cool glass and focusing on nothing in particular as I gazed out over the courtyard. Then a glimmer of movement caught my eye and I snapped alert. There was a figure in the courtyard, their form shrouded in fog. For a heart-stopping moment I was sure it was the man in the black trenchcoat, whoever he was. Then the mist swirled away on an updraft and I recognized her.

As I stood in the window, gawking in surprise, she lifted her face toward the light and our eyes met.

I turned away from the window, taking a few deep breaths. Then I pulled the blinds down and went downstairs.

I slipped out into the courtyard, my breath coming out in puffs that swirled into the heavy fog. I found her sitting on the wrought iron bench. I hesitated a moment, thinking about how wet my butt was going to get, before shrugging and sitting down beside her.

I watched her for a minute while she avoided my eyes. "So," I said finally, when it became clear that she wasn't planning on being the first one to speak, "mind telling me what you're doing here creeping outside my house?"

Shailene reached into her pocket, withdrawing something and handing it to me, still not looking at me. My phone.

"Janice didn't get a chance to give you that back before... whatever. So I told her I'd take care of it."

I quirked an eyebrow. "That was nice of you."

She shrugged. Her gaze was fixed on the letters mounted on the brick wall. "You don't seem like you'd be a sorority girl."

I opened my mouth to give her my go-to speech about how Gam-Lam is a multicultural sorority, not a social one, but the words died on my lips. Somehow I didn't think Shailene would care about the distinction. So I just said, "Well, you don't seem like you'd be a cheerleader."

She smirked, and I knew I'd said the right thing. "Touché." She hunched forward, leaning her elbows on her knees, and finally looked at me sidelong. "Listen, Laura," she said, "I know I've been kind of an asshole to you."

I snorted, trying to ignore the way my stomach flip-flopped when she looked at me like that. "That's one way to put it."

She pursed her lips, a gesture that on her came off more elegant than petulant. "Yeah, yeah, I get it. But look at it from my point of view. You turn up out of nowhere, and all of a sudden my friends start going missing. More than just my friends, my—my teammates." Her face had that pained expression on it again, and I realized that these girls were more to her than just fellow cheerleaders. That might have seemed strange to me if not for the fact that I was in a sorority. I knew, even without her saying it, how much things can change when you spend so much time together. I wondered how I would react if something happened to my big.

Shailene leaned back against the bench. She felt warm beside me, a respite from the chill in the air around us. "This wasn't supposed to happen. Yeah, the Anesidorans had us all once. But when the I.G.A. gets you out, that's supposed to be it. They're not supposed to get you again. Especially not if you're on our level. If you're a Striker. Sentries are slow and dumb. They've never been able to catch up... before."

"So what changed?" I asked.

She let her breath out in a long, heavy sigh. "I don't know. The whole world's gone crazy. Something happened the day you turned up."

"Do you think I had something to do with it?" I was almost afraid to hear the answer.

"I don't know," she repeated. "Something about it's different. But... I don't believe you *mean* to have anything to do with it, even if you do."

"Thanks, I guess." I looked down at my hands, light-brown and ordinary, short nails covered in peeling nail decals and chipped polish. I didn't feel any different. But I was. I must have been. If I was a part of this weird other world, did it mean I had powers, too? How had I not noticed them before?

"Shailene," I said, "if I was... modified... and no one told me... How would I know?"

She frowned. "If you'd been abducted, you'd know it. There's no forgetting that."

"But what if it was someone in my family? One of my parents?"

Shailene glanced down at her own hands. "It's possible. It's happened before, albeit rarely. The I.G.A. has done its best to keep track of all the families of lab rats that we have records of. But there are a few who have slipped through, especially if the ancestor was one of the early experiments. Sometimes the modified traits become recessive genes, not turning up until generations later."

"And what happens to those people?"

"Usually it starts with them seeing things that aren't there. Hearing voices that no one else can hear. In the old days, they'd get locked in an asylum. It can be hard to tell the difference between someone with a medical condition like schizophrenia and someone who can actually see *more* than they should."

I shivered, only partly from the cold.

"Anesidorans are good at disguising themselves," Shailene said. "But the experiments can see past their cloaking devices, hear the sounds that carry at that frequency. It's like everyone around you is blind, and you're the only one with a working pair of glasses or something. That's usually the first sign that someone's different. We *perceive*. It's the hardest power to control, to shut out. The other traits we have—speed, strength—they have to be developed. You usually can't tap into them unless you consciously try. You usually don't know you can do it... until you actually do."

Again with the cryptic stuff. I sighed. "What's that supposed to mean, exactly?"

She looked uncomfortable. "Let's just say, you don't want to make a repressed experiment angry."

I winced. "Let me guess: Hulk smash?"

"That's one way to put it."

We sat there quietly for a long moment, tendrils of fog snaking around me, freezing my ears and my fingers and my toes.

"Shailene," I said at last, so softly I could barely hear myself, "I... I want to help you. I know what my dad said, but I also know that whatever's going on, I'm a part of it. I can't just do nothing." I turned toward her as I spoke, my bare knee lightly brushing against hers. At the contact, that same sharp pain came back, stabbing between my eyes. In my ears, a girl's laugh echoed, familiar and foreign all at once. My fingers tingled with the memory of a warm hand entwined with mine.

I gasped, and next to me I felt Shailene recoil.

"You feel that, too?" she hissed between clenched teeth.

I nodded, rubbing my eyes with the heel of my hand. "Every time..." I trailed off, my face hot.

"Every time we touch," Shailene finished quietly. I could feel the telltale blush on my cheeks, and I wondered if she noticed my disappointment at the confirmation of my suspicion. Getting a migraine every time you touch is not exactly helpful if you're trying to put the moves on someone—which I definitely hadn't been planning on, regardless. Obviously.

But it was still damned inconvenient.

Shailene stood, pulling her letterman jacket tighter around her shoulders. "You're right," she said. "Something is going on here. You are a part of this. Everything that's happened in the past two days has proved that. And I can't get rid of this feeling that I know you, but every time I try to reach for it..." She squeezed her eyes shut, then opened them. "But whatever it is, it's something we're not supposed to know. Something that could get us in trouble."

She was pulling away from me, retreating into her shell. I could *feel* her putting a wall up between us. It was like she was cutting me off from her in a way I hadn't even realized existed until it was removed. I wondered if this was what she'd meant by perception.

"Wait, so that's just it?" I spluttered. "You have a *feeling* that we know each other, but we're not supposed to question how or why neither of us can remember it, because you have another *feeling* that we shouldn't?"

She rolled her eyes. "It's more than that."

"Really? Then please elaborate. Because I think we both have a right to know what's going on here."

"Laura, look." She was staring at the letters on the house again, stubbornly avoiding my gaze. "I have orders. We're not supposed to come around you anymore. Even if I want to find out the truth—and I do—I can't go against orders."

"Oh, of course. Your orders. Never mind the fact that someone's obviously been screwing around in our brains and we don't know why. Never mind the fact that you just told me two minutes ago that if I have powers—which I know I do—and if I don't learn to control them, I could accidentally kill someone."

Her expression cracked, for just a fraction of a second. "It's not under my control."

I stood up, too. As predicted, my butt was soaked. I tried not to let it faze me. "Okay, got it. Whatever, Shailene. Follow your orders. But do it for real this time. *Actually* leave me alone. No more creeping on me outside my sorority house, or stalking me at restaurants."

Now she did look at me. "I didn't—"

"No, I don't want to hear it. I'm leaving now. Goodbye."

I turned hotly on my heel and stormed back into the house, not caring even if she did see the huge wet splotch on my pajama shorts. I wouldn't let her see me act self-conscious. The door swung slowly closed behind me, the pneumatic hinge on it preventing me the satisfaction of slamming it. Once it was shut, I leaned back against it, taking several deep breaths, trying to calm down. Trying not to cry.

Back in my room, I stared at the closed window for a long moment. Then I lifted one of the blinds the tiniest fraction, peeking down into the yard.

The courtyard was empty.

- Chapter 7 -

So, in the night, I'd reached a few conclusions.

The first was that I was relatively certain that my dad was completely lying to me about not being an abductee. It was the only thing that made sense. I knew *I* wasn't an abductee, but he had been involved with the I.G.A. just like all the other rescued lab rats. Out of everyone in my family, my dad was the logical choice.

The second was that there was no way in hell I was just going to stay out of it. Regardless of what Dad said, regardless of what Shailene said, even if the Anesidorans weren't actively trying to harm me, they had definitely been following me since Thursday. I couldn't just sit around and do nothing until they decided that just watching me was getting dull and decided to fry my brain or something. If I had powers, I needed to learn how to use them. I needed to be able to protect myself.

And the third conclusion I'd reached was that Ana had probably slept with her mystery date last night. She certainly hadn't come home. I knew this because I couldn't sleep at all after Shailene had left. I'd stayed up all night, actually finishing my English paper. Every time I'd heard a noise I'd jumped up and looked out the window, but while the rest of the Deltas had staggered in around two A.M., Ana had been a no-show. And this morning when I'd checked her room, her bed had still been neatly made.

Whoever this guy was, he'd better be worth it.

The kitchenette was empty at seven o'clock when I made my way downstairs, so I was able to fry an egg without having to compete with anyone for the hot plate. The big kitchen, with its actual gas stove rather than this pathetic electric burner, would be locked until our house mom got back from vacation tomorrow night. Because apparently we couldn't be trusted to not burn the house down. I scarfed down the egg with a not-too-stale pandesal roll out of the freezer and some coffee to wake me up. Then I threw on some lip gloss and my ass-kickingest pair of boots and headed out into the cold morning fog.

The first order of business, I'd decided during the night, was to try to get a handle on what powers I might have to begin with. Shailene had neglected to explain whether every abductee—or abductee's kid, in my case—had the same abilities, or if we were looking at an X-Men-style situation where everyone could do something different. If that was the case, knowing my luck, I'd wind up like Zeitgeist and his acid puke rather than having something cool like weather control or laser beam eyes.

But there was one thing I knew for sure I did have: perception. I could see things I wasn't supposed to, that much was clear. But I could also *feel* things, something I hadn't even realized until last night when Shailene had blocked me. And I remembered what she'd said when the girl in the alley had disappeared—*"I can't sense her anywhere."* If the cheerleaders could sense each other, maybe I could sense them, too. If I could track down the missing girls, maybe it would show Janice Sheldon that she could trust me, regardless of what my dad said. And then I could get to the bottom of what was happening to me, and why.

Outside, the world was quiet apart from the erratic noises of early morning traffic, and even that was muted in the dense fog. I shied away from the bench where Shailene and I had sat last night, and instead made my way to the far side of the courtyard, where a massive blue gum tree towered over the waist-high brick wall separating Gam-Lam from the street. The wall was uneven in parts where the massive roots of the tree had displaced the ground beneath it. I often heard people complaining about how the sidewalk outside was a tripping hazard because of it, but I didn't mind. I loved that the tree had made itself comfortable here.

I placed a hand on the tree trunk and breathed in through my nose, letting myself savor the scent of it for just a moment. I loved the way this tree smelled, sort of minty with a hint of honey. We had a ton of eucalyptus trees growing on our property in Everett; the previous owner had planted them as a windbreak. They reminded me of home.

I stared up, focusing on the budding white flowers high over my head, the peeling bark in the upper branches, and the waxy blue baby leaves clustered among the deep green grownups. Then, slowly, I closed my eyes.

Concentrate, Laura. Be at peace. Be Aang. I tried not to snort at the thought. I was definitely not an Aang—I was a Korra, through and through. *But, hey,* I reminded myself, *Korra made it in the end. Saved the day, got the girl. Be Korra if you need to be.*

Eyes still closed, I stretched my mind, trying to focus on the feeling I'd had the night before, just before Shailene cut me off. *Think of the cheerleaders. Think of the girl on the skateboard, or the one on the scooter. Think of green eyes, red lightning, trains moving so fast...*

Nothing. I sighed, opening my eyes and leaning back against the gum tree. Maybe this was too advanced for me. Even Shailene hadn't been able to find the girls after they'd vanished. Maybe—

I swallowed hard, not wanting to follow the path my thoughts were wandering down. There could be a million reasons why Shailene couldn't sense the missing cheerleaders. It didn't necessarily mean that they were no longer on this mortal plane. They'd just been taken out of range, that's all. Been beamed up to the mother ship.

I'd try a different tactic. Maybe the missing girls weren't on Earth anymore, but Anesidorans were. Their sentries were all around, hiding in plain sight. If I tracked them down, maybe I could follow them to the missing girls. I just needed to find one of those bug things, or maybe—

Unbidden, the man in the black trenchcoat popped into my mind. I shuddered, remembering the way his skin had oscillated rainbow colors in my dream like a damn disco ball.

And then there it was. Bam. It wasn't quite like radar; it was more like that feeling you get when someone's been staring at you across the room and you suddenly notice it. Just like that, I knew he was there. I knew where he was.

Before I could think twice, I was off. I dashed out from

under the eucalyptus tree and through the gate, running down the sidewalk, jumping nimbly over the uneven section behind the tree. My mind was completely blank. I was afraid that if I let myself think of anything else, I'd lose my slippery grasp on this feeling and then I'd never be able to find him.

The wind whipped past me as I ran, mist swirling in my wake. I felt like I was moving faster than normal, though maybe it was just an illusion because of the fog. I was almost on him now. I could feel him on the next street over, standing right in front of—

I barreled around the corner and nearly slammed into a couple standing on the sidewalk. I skidded to a halt, losing my balance on the stupid wedge heels on my black leather boots. My hands flailed in front of me as I teetered, struggling to keep from falling. "I'm sorry, I'm sorry!" I blurted.

"Whoa, are you okay?" a guy's voice asked, and a tan hand reached out to brace me, just grazing the side of my arm long enough to steady me.

"Yeah, I'm fi—Ana!" I gasped, finally looking up long enough to notice who was standing in front of me.

The world seemed to screech to a halt as I gawked at the two of them, my mouth flapping open and closed soundlessly like a fish. In what felt like slow motion, I looked back and forth between them and the house we were standing in front of, a stucco behemoth that displayed typical frat house slovenry: a worn-out couch on the roof, perfect for viewing Mariner football games without leaving the house; tied-up black garbage bags sitting on the front doorstep, probably from last Friday's mixer, waiting for someone to give up and take them out to the dumpster; and the copper letters *Beta Eta Beta* mounted over the front door, half-oxidized into a sea-green patina that I'm sure the designer thought would look cool but just seemed to give the impression this was less a house and more an abandoned tenement that college guys had wandered into like rats, slapped some rusty letters on and established residency in.

None of this, incidentally, is meant to be a disparagement of frat guys. Tonio was a Phi Kap, after all. It's just an unbiased description of their living conditions, which, undeniably, are more often than not completely atrocious.

You'd never know it from looking at the guy standing in front of me now, though. He looked like a model for Abercrombie & Fitch. He had to be a full foot taller than me, and his perfectly square jaw was clean-shaven, showing only the slightest hint of neatly-groomed stubble. His thick black hair was styled in a way that reminded me of '90s boy bands—loaded with gel, not a hair out of place. He was possibly part Asian; apart from the dated hairstyle, he kind of had the look of a K-Pop star. I could smell his Acqua di Gio from five feet away. He wore a trim camel hair coat, but his broad shoulders indicated that he was probably pretty buff under those long sleeves.

And his long, tan fingers were entwined in Ana's.

"Laura," Ana said. She was totally blushing, but her dark complexion hid it well. I'd always been jealous of my full-Pinoy relatives about this. With my mom's pale-ass skin and my dad being white, I never stood a chance. I go redder than a tomato at the drop of a hat. "What are you doing here?" she stammered. "Usually you sleep in on the weekend."

"I had a headache last night, so I went to bed before nine," I lied. "Figured I'd get up early and get some jogging in." She stared at my very-jogging-inappropriate motorcycle boots in confusion. I quickly changed the subject, looking up at the giant Beta before me. "I don't think we've met. I'm Laura, Ana's little in Gam-Lam."

"Oh, sorry," Ana said hurriedly. "Laura, this is Damien, my..."

She trailed off, looking uncertain, and he grinned, showing off a mouth of perfectly straight white teeth.

"Your boyfriend, right?"

Ana exhaled, smiling sheepishly. "Yeah. My boyfriend." Damien laughed and put his arm around her shoulder. My stomach twisted ever so slightly.

"Anyway, Laura, it's so great to finally meet you," he said, sticking his right hand out for me to shake. "Ana's told me so much about you."

Stiffly, I took it. "Really? That's a surprise, considering that she's told me absolutely nothing about you." As soon as I said it, I regretted it, but there was no taking it back. Damien's face fell like I'd slapped him across the face. Ana looked down at her feet. Flustered, I tried to recover. "I mean, not like she's had a chance. You guys haven't known each other that long, right? Makeisha said you met at the mixer last week."

"Well, not quite," Damien said. He smiled in a more cordial—and forced—way than he had a moment ago. "That's when I asked her out. We've had class together before, since we're both bio majors."

"Oh," I said awkwardly.

"Damien wants to be a veterinarian, too," Ana added, cheerfully trying to cover up the disaster I'd made of this encounter.

He wanted to be a vet. No wonder she liked him. I

smiled in a way I hoped seemed friendly. "That's great. Ana loves animals. This one time a stray dog had puppies in the service alley behind our house, and she sneaked her and the puppies in and managed to keep it a secret from our house mom for a month until she rehomed all of them."

Ana laughed. "Well, I still think Claudia knew about it and just kept her mouth shut. They were so cute, I couldn't just leave them."

Damien was beaming at Ana in a nauseating way. I gnawed on the inside of my cheek. Why did I have to run into them now? I had more important things to do this morning than watch this wannabe from a teen drama circa *before I was born* macking on my big. Every minute that I wasted here, Trenchcoat Guy was getting farther away.

As if my thoughts had summoned him, suddenly I sensed him again. And he wasn't farther—he was closer. Just a few blocks away. I couldn't lose him now.

Distantly, I heard rap music start to play. A cell phone ringing. Not mine, though. I closed my eyes, trying to block out the sounds of the world around me, focus on the man I was tracking.

The park. That's where he was heading. For a brief instant I could see the duck pond in my mind, the art deco architecture of the children's museum, the bronze glint of the flame on Firebelle Tower peeking over the trees. He was waiting for someone.

"Laura?"

I blinked as the sound of Ana's voice snapped me back to reality. "What? Sorry, I spaced for a second."

Damien had moved a few feet away from us, holding his phone to his ear.

"I said we're going to get breakfast when he's off the phone, if you want to come?"

"Oh. I—that is—"

And then my breath caught in my throat as I finally sensed who he was waiting for. A petite, dark-skinned girl with braids pulled back with a thick scrunchie. She was close. And she was walking right into his trap.

Erikka. It was Erikka Johnson. And if I didn't get to her before he did, she'd disappear, too.

"I'm sorry, Ana," I blurted, barely registering the surprise on her face. "Maybe another time? I mean, really. I'm not just saying that. I really do want to. I just—I have to go."

"Laura?"

I ducked my head, fingers to my lips in apology. "Seriously, I'm sorry! I'll text you!" Before she could react, I was off again, tearing past Damien, who lowered his phone away from his ear for just a second to look at me in confusion. I thought I heard him say my name, but I didn't answer.

I had to hurry. Erikka was moving toward the park fast. If I didn't get there first, there was no telling what would happen.

Run, Laura. Faster. Like you know you can.

The muscles in my legs pumped, but it still wasn't fast enough. Not Anesidoran fast. Just human fast. Come on, Laura, you can do this. You *have* to do this.

I focused on the man in my mind, the girl moving toward him. I let the thought of them consume my entire brain.

And then I ran.

I thought it had seemed like I was moving too fast before, but now I knew I was. The street blurred past me like I was in a car, but it was just me, running on the sidewalk. I wondered if anyone could see me, what they would think if they could. But then I remembered the girl on the skateboard, the one only I could see. Maybe it was like that, like Shailene had said. *No one can see them because they don't* want *to be seen.*

I could only pray that was true.

Lillian Brown Park was a sprawling sea of green in the middle of a concrete jungle, a small valley nestled in between the rolling hills that the City had been built upon.

At over five hundred acres, it was the biggest park in the east ward, and second biggest in the metro area, matched only by its twin in City West. Dozens of walking trails crisscrossed in between massive oak and eucalyptus trees, lush gardens and picnic pavilions. It wasn't too busy yet, this early in the morning, but the sun was starting to burn the fog away, and scattered joggers and power-walkers dotted the sidewalks.

I dodged to avoid them as I ran. People didn't seem to react to the blur racing past them, but I wasn't sure if I could still collide with them—and at this speed, I didn't want to take the risk. I felt off-balance, weaving in between throngs of pedestrians. It was like trying to slalom ski when you've only ever been on the bunny slopes. The motorcycle boots weren't helping, either. I should have stuck with sneakers.

As I zigzagged around a pack of marathon trainers, a sudden wave of nausea struck me. I was flagging, big time. I'd never run this far this fast, and it was catching up to me. *Hang in there, Laura*, I thought. I was almost to the duck pond. If I could just...

And then my ankle rolled.

I fell hard, face-planting onto the sidewalk and half-skidding, half-tumbling off the path into the bushes. The shock of the impact knocked the wind clean out of me. I lay there in the mud for a moment, panting, as my muscles tingled like sand was running through my veins, and speckles shimmered in front of my eyes.

"Whoa, are you okay?" a girl's voice asked. She ran over and crouched beside me. As my vision swam and cleared, I realized it was Erikka. I blinked. Just over her shoulder, I could see the branches of the willow trees that grew at the pond's edge.

"Erikka," I said, my voice ragged. I wasn't too late. I could still save her.

She stared at me in bewilderment for a moment, and then recognition dawned on her. "Laura Clark. What are you doing here? We're not—"

"Erikka, listen to me," I said. "You have to be careful. It's a trap. He's—"

"There you are."

My breath caught in my throat at the sound of his voice. Silky-smooth, almost debonair. Erikka stiffened, whirling to face him, crouched on the balls of her heels.

"Striker," the man in the trenchcoat said, stepping forward, his arms folded. It was the first time I'd gotten a good look at him. He was older, maybe somewhere between my mom's age and Lola's. He had a square jaw, and fair skin that looked almost like porcelain, with narrow green eyes that sparked as he looked at us. "I've been expecting you. You always come when I call."

I furrowed my brows. He'd called her? What was that supposed to mean?

Erikka clenched her fist. "I don't know what you're talking about."

He chuckled. "They never do. And the explanations are getting tedious, so never mind. It's time for you to come with me."

"I'm not going anywhere with you." She unzipped her jacket, withdrawing something that looked suspiciously like a pair of nunchakus. She was going to fight him.

The man in the trenchcoat sighed. "That's what they all say. But they all come in the end."

"Don't fight him," I whispered, pushing myself up onto my knees. I still felt weak and shaky, and my hands were numb like they'd fallen asleep. "That's how the others disappeared. You need to run, Erikka."

"Strikers don't run," she replied.

"Erikka, please—"

Without another word, she sprang forward, whipping her nunchakus around like freaking Bruce Lee or something. Trenchcoat Guy dodged her faster than my eyes could keep up, skirting back through the trees toward the water.

"Wait!" I gasped, struggling to my feet and running after them. Erikka kept advancing, the man expertly evading each of her assaults, leading her forward, across the bridge, farther away from me. She lashed out with her weapons once more, and this time after he dodged, he lunged forward, capturing her wrist in his and dragging her close to him. Before she could react, he clamped his right hand over her eyes.

Lightning struck.

I screamed, toppling back into the bushes as the red light blinded me, filling the air everywhere around me and making my vision flash once more. I blinked violently, trying to clear the spots from my eyes.

I heard them before I could see again. "That's more like it," the man's smooth, deep voice said.

I blinked again, and there they were, still standing on the bridge. They hadn't disappeared this time. Not yet at least. Erikka had dropped her nunchakus, and she stared at her hands now, as if she were confused by their existence.

"How do you feel?" the man asked.

Erikka looked up at him slowly, her head cocked. "Better," she replied.

He smiled, his lips thin. "Good. Let's go."

He turned, starting across the bridge once more, away from me. Erikka walked beside him freely, no sign of resistance. They walked slowly, casually, but their movement didn't match their motions. Each step seemed to take them the distance of ten. I stared after their rapidly disappearing forms, my mind reeling. "Wait," I said after a moment, my voice hoarse, barely audible. Then I shakily rose to my feet, running after them across the bridge. "Wait!"

I tried to keep up, tried to will myself to find the speed I'd had earlier, but my legs refused to cooperate. They wobbled and shook as I ran, barely as fast as I could normally manage. My breath was painful and sharp, scraping at my lungs with each inhalation.

Within seconds, Erikka and the man were out of my view, but I refused to stop. I closed my eyes, reaching out with my mind. Erikka was gone. It was like she was invisible, like she'd closed me off the way Shailene had last night. But I could still feel Trenchcoat Guy, and I clung to him with all my might. I wouldn't lose him. I couldn't.

I was out of the valley now, at the far eastern edge of the park where the trees tapered off, the ground began to slope and the sidewalks turned to steps. The fog was completely gone now, and Firebelle Tower rose above me, a massive concrete torch with bronze flames that burned bright in the sunlight. This was the park's end; a large retaining wall separated it from the rest of the city, but I could hear the noises from the street beyond. Erikka and the man in the trenchcoat were far past here. They were disappearing into the city.

I pushed myself forward, starting up the steps in front of the tower. I wouldn't stop. I had to keep going.

I had to keep going.

I cleared the last steps, rounding the foot of the tower, and collided with someone.

"Laura Clark," a woman's voice said, and hands grabbed my shoulders, keeping me from pitching backward. "I thought that was you running up those stairs like a bat out of hell. What on earth are you doing here?"

I blinked the sun out of my eyes, thinking to myself that this was the third time I had *literally* run into someone I knew in the last hour, and I'd had about enough of it. Then I realized who was standing in front of me, and relief overwhelmed me.

Janice Sheldon. She was wearing a bright pink T-shirt with a denim jacket over it, her long, blond hair pulled back in a ponytail once more. Behind her, Shailene hovered, watching me without coming too close.

"Janice," I panted. "It's Erikka. He has Erikka."

She blinked at me, as if she was having trouble understanding what I was saying. "What?"

"The guy who took the others. Weirdo in a black fedora

and a long coat."

"That's what I was trying to tell you, Coach," Shailene said quietly, still standing a distance away. "Erikka and I were doing our warm-ups, but then she took off. I can't feel her anymore."

Janice's expression was unreadable. "Oh, my God," she breathed. "You were following him, Laura?"

"Yeah." I put my hands on my knees, breathing hard. I felt kind of like I was going to throw up. "But I couldn't keep up. I can barely feel him now. He's still close, but he's getting away."

Janice turned to Shailene. "Get her a Gatorade. There's some in the car. The electrolytes will help." Shailene scurried away, and Janice crouched down in front of me. "Are you telling me that you can sense this man?"

"Yes." I heaved. "Or, at least, I could. I'm having trouble finding him now."

"You overdid it," she said, putting a steadying hand on my shoulder. "You have to learn to control your energy expenditure. Just because we're superhuman doesn't mean we're unstoppable."

"Well, how the hell should I know?" I snapped. "No one is willing to explain anything to me. I've been having to figure it all out myself." I squeezed my eyes shut, straining, trying desperately to hold onto the thread of connection between me and the man in the trenchcoat. But it was gone. He was gone. "I've lost him," I whispered.

"It's okay. You'll find him again," Janice said.

Shailene reappeared then, holding a plastic bottle. Janice took it from her, cracking the seal and handing it to me. I drank deeply.

Janice watched me for a moment, then rose. "All right," she said, looking between me and Shailene. "Change of plans. We're going against orders."

Shailene's eyebrows rose. "What? But, Coach—"

"This is an emergency, Shai. Our team is almost gone. If Laura thinks she can help us find them—and I believe she can—and she's willing to help us, then we need her help."

I thought for a second that Shailene was going to argue with her. But she just quirked her mouth and nodded.

I put the cap back on the bottle and shakily straightened. "Seriously? You're going to let me come with you?"

"Yes," Janice said. "And we'll show you how to control these powers of yours, so that you don't overextend yourself again."

I grinned. "Great. Thank you." I hesitated, then added,

"And you won't tell my dad, right?"

She leveled a look at me, a sort of mischief in her hazel eyes that seemed to hint at something she wouldn't quite say. "I wouldn't dream of it."

- Chapter 8 -

I leaned back against the concrete balustrade, my eyes closed, breathing in the smell of eucalyptus leaves on the slightly salty breeze blowing off the bay. The air was fresh around the park, and especially up here, away from the exhaust fumes from traffic down at ground level. The bright morning sun warmed the skin on my forearms deliciously. *Janice was right*, I thought, opening my eyes and looking up at the blue sky. *The sun really does help.*

After I'd downed a full bottle of orange sports drink (and a yogurt smoothie, and two granola bars—they kept shoving food at me, and I wasn't about to complain), Janice had said, "We need to get to higher ground. She needs light to help her regain her energy, and if she's going to track this Anesidoran man, she needs as few obstructions as possible.

There's too much interference at street level. The best place for sensing is above."

Shailene glanced up at Firebelle Tower looming over our heads. "Up there?"

Janice nodded. "As good a place as any. We probably shouldn't leave this area until we know for sure where they're going. We could inadvertently move away from them, and then she'd never get his signal back."

"Hold up now," I said, following Shailene's gaze. "We can't go up *there*. That's not a tower for people to go up, it's a tower for people to look at from the ground. I don't think there's even a way to go inside it, and even if there were, it's definitely off-limits to random college students. And what's this about needing light? What am I, some kind of plant?"

"The rules don't apply to us, in case you hadn't noticed," said Janice. "And yes, plant photosynthesis is a good comparison. Though all humans do need sunshine. Ever heard of a little thing called 'Vitamin-D deficiency'?"

I took a deep breath, looking up at the massive tower above us, a slender pillar of smooth concrete that rose a good fifty feet before being topped with brilliant bronze flames. "Okay, I'll bite," I said. "How are we supposed to get up there, though?" I remembered Joanie, the cheerleader with the green eyes on the side of the train on

Thursday, and how she seemed to cling to its sides with no support like a Human Fly. Was that one of our powers?

Shailene smirked, seeming to read my mind. "You don't have to climb it. There's a service entrance around the back. Those flames don't stay that shiny on their own. I mean, unless you *want* to climb it," she added, a devious grin quirking the corners of her lips.

"No, no, I'm good," I said quickly. "Don't want to overdo it or anything."

They led me to small balcony at the top of the stairs, a narrow concrete outcropping that emerged between the jagged flames, invisible from ground level. "There," Janice said, looking around in satisfaction. "Laura, you try to rest. Roll up your sleeves, let the sun hit you, and focus your mind. See if you can pick up on that man's signal again. Shailene, I'm going to get the amplifier. Keep an eye on her, okay?"

Shailene made a noncommittal noise and climbed up over the balustrade and into the flames, perching herself about fifteen feet away from me. I watched her for a minute, pulling the motorcycle boots off my aching feet and stretching my bare toes. "Isn't that metal hot?" I asked her.

"Not really," she said.

Janice looked between us for a minute and sighed. "I'll be right back. Try not to get into any trouble."

And so we'd sat in complete silence until now. Every so often I could feel Shailene looking over at me from where she was roosting like the goddamn Batman, but I stubbornly avoided her gaze. When I opened my eyes, I stared out over the park, across the City toward the Bay. From up here, you could see everything—all the way to City West, its tall buildings bisected with its own strip of green marking Jones Park and the City Zoo.

In my pocket, my phone buzzed, accompanied by the "secret" noise from *The Legend of Zelda*—my message alert tone. Out of the corner of my eye, I saw Shailene grin. I ignored her and pulled my phone out.

It was a text from Ana. *Hey, everything ok?* she'd written.

I shifted awkwardly, feeling Shailene watching me still. *Yeah, it's fine*, I typed.

A few seconds later, my phone buzzed again. *Good. Damien was sorry you couldn't come to breakfast. Maybe dinner tonight?*

I stared down at my phone, my stomach knotting up again, not knowing how to respond. Why did I feel this way? It wasn't like I was jealous. I'd never had a crush on Ana—on top of the fact that she's straight, she's like family. The thought of that was as gross as the thought of having a crush on Tonio or something. But it didn't change the fact that the thought of her dating this *NSYNC wannabe with his fancy hair and freakishly perfect teeth made me want to cry. Or barf. Not necessarily in that order.

I sighed and shoved my phone back in my pocket.

"Everything okay?" Shailene asked, echoing Ana's words.

"It's fine," I said.

Shailene was quiet for a moment, crouched with her arms draped across her knees, looking down at her hands. "It seems like no matter how hard I try, I'm always sticking my foot in my mouth around you."

"What?" I said, not sure I'd heard her right.

She shrugged. "Like yesterday. I'm sure you spent all last night thinking about what a bitch I am."

I blinked rapidly, looking away. "Actually, no. I didn't think about you at all last night after you left." It was a total lie—that was exactly what I'd done, but I didn't want her to *know* that.

She laughed awkwardly. "Of course not." Something in her tone of voice made me glance back at her. Her face was bright red. "There I go, foot in mouth again. Never mind. Forget I said anything."

We sat in uncomfortable silence. After a moment,

Shailene stood, pacing across the angled metal plating of the torch's flames. She had some good balance—and nerves of steel—to walk around out there, I thought. She pulled at her long, dark hair as she paced, twisting it up into a bun, knotting it into itself. That's when I noticed—at the nape of her neck was a small tattoo, slightly smudged at the edges with age. An inverted black triangle.

"Your tattoo," I said hesitantly.

She looked at me, her eyes guarded. "What about it?"

I shrugged. "I like it. I was just going to say I have a similar one." I pulled up the cuff of my jeans, revealing a small heart on my ankle, emblazoned with the rainbow pride flag.

Something in her eyes changed at the sight of it. Softened a little. For a brief second, I felt that wall that she'd built between us last night start to crumble—just a bit. "Oh," she said. "That's cool."

I smiled in what I hoped was a conciliatory fashion, and she smiled back. We looked out over the treetops together.

"I've always loved this place," she finally said.

I grinned, eager to have a conversation with her that didn't involve us arguing. "Yeah? Do you come here often?"

"Yeah. It's a good place to monitor Anesidoran activity.

There's not as much interference with the amplifier. But... sometimes I just come here. You know. To think."

"No good thinking spots in City West?" I teased.

She half-turned, glancing up at the glinting flames rising over us. "It's not that. It's more like... I feel a connection to this place. Do you know the story of Firebelle Lil?"

"Lillian Brown?" I clarified. "A little. I know that she was the first female firefighter in the City, back in the early nineteen-hundreds." This tower was built as a memorial to her—there was a plaque saying so down at the base—and the park was named after her, too.

"Those are the basics," Shailene said. "But there's more to it. This tower was donated to the city by Sylvester Jones, the newspaper mogul."

"The guy the park in City West is named after."

"Yeah. Sylvester Jones was in love with Firebelle Lil, and he asked her to marry him at least half a dozen times. But she always turned him down. After she died in the Great Fire, he had this tower built in her memory and donated it to the City as part of the park." She ran a hand thoughtfully along the smooth, gleaming bronze. "But that's not the whole story. The real reason she turned him down is because"—she hesitated, seeming unsure if she should continue; but then her eyes flashed, determined—

"she already had a lover. A woman named Betty."

My heart skipped slightly, both from Shailene's words and the way she looked at me when she said them. This was something I'd never known. Firebelle Lil was one of the great heroes of the City. She'd saved hundreds of lives before the flames had taken her own. I'd heard about her all my life, but I'd never heard that she might have been a lesbian. "Is that true?"

"It's true," Shailene said. "I found a book in the library that had some of their letters in it, Lillian and Betty's. Believe me, there was nothing platonic about them. But they neglect to mention that in history class, huh?" She smiled wryly. "Anyway, that's why... Firebelle Lil is kind of special to me. I used to come here a lot when I was... going through some stuff. I feel closer to her here. Even if this tower *was* built by a more-than-slightly-obsessive straight guy who couldn't take a hint."

I laughed, and Shailene laughed with me. It felt nice to not be at odds with her.

And familiar.

I chewed on the inside of my cheek, thinking. "Listen, Shailene," I began, "I know you said you felt like we shouldn't push things—like maybe we weren't *supposed* to know—but don't you think..."

The service doorway opened just then, cutting me off. Janice came out onto the balcony, her arms laden with equipment I could only guess the purpose of.

"Right, Laura," she said, setting a large black plastic-and-metal box down against the balustrade, "how are you feeling?"

I blinked. "Better, actually." And I did. I hadn't noticed, but I'd felt tangibly better since Shailene had started talking to me.

"Good. Then let's get this set up. It's an amplifier. It boosts our sensing range. Hopefully it will work for you. I'm not sure why you're able to sense this man when none of us are"—she glanced at me sideways for a moment—"but at this point, I don't care. If it works, if it can get our girls back, I'll take it."

"Okay," I said, watching her open the box and fiddle with some diodes. It looked like a piece of stereo equipment. Janice pulled out two long rabbit-ear antennas, adjusting them slightly while looking at a small digital reader on the box's face.

"So, who is this guy I'm tracking, anyway?" I asked as she fiddled with the controls.

"From your description, it sounds like Andronicus," Janice replied. She turned a dial, eyes still riveted to the digital screen. "He's a high-ranking official on Nibiru, one of the commanders of the Anesidoran fleet."

I chewed my lip, remembering the way he'd seemed to be watching me over the past two days. What would someone like that be interested in me for? "None of the other abductees are able to sense him?"

"Not that I'm aware of. He operates on a different frequency from us, if you will."

I swallowed, looking back out at the park. "So why can I?" I whispered.

I didn't realize she'd heard me, but she shook her head. "That's the million-dollar question." She flipped a switch and looked at me. "There. All set."

"That's it?" I didn't notice any change.

"That's it. Try to see if you can get a reading on him now."

"All right, I guess," I said uncertainly. I didn't know how this thing was supposed to help me when I didn't feel any different. Was I supposed to be like a bat now, able to hear radar or something?

Shailene jumped back onto the balcony and smiled reassuringly at me. I smiled back, hoping I wasn't blushing too much. Then I closed my eyes, reaching out with my mind. Listening, almost.

"I don't know," I started. "I don't see how—" I broke off abruptly. Out of nowhere, I felt him. He was far away, a lot farther than he'd been when I'd sensed him at the park. So distant I could barely feel him at all. But there, in fragments, I saw it. The mall in the Hilltop district, with its tall Gothic clock tower. An old-fashioned trolley car dinged as it went by, slowly plodding its way up the steepest hill in the city. Across the street from the mall was the massive Union Station, where all four PeRT lines converged along with an Amtrak station and the Greyhound bus. It was the central location for anyone going in and out of the City.

And suddenly I knew, beyond a shadow of a doubt, that they were leaving. He was taking Erikka out of the City.

"Union Station," I said, opening my eyes and looking from Janice to Shailene. "And we have to hurry. We don't have much time."

"Right," Janice said. "You sure you're feeling all right, Laura?"

"Yeah. I feel good."

"Okay, then. You're about to get your first crash course in Striker 101: moving fast."

"Moving fast I can do," I said, pulling my boots back on. "I figured that one out this morning."

"Good. We'll put that to the test." Janice unzipped a black backpack that lay beside the amplifier, rummaging through it and withdrawing a pair of black fingerless gloves. She tossed them to me. "You'll need these."

"And these are?"

"Your Human Fly gloves," Shailene said, giving me a wink that made my stomach flip-flop. "Or would you prefer Spider-Man?"

"Not unless they let me shoot webs and fly around New York City," I replied in what I hoped was a level voice.

"Afraid not," said Janice. She slung the backpack over her shoulders, pulling the straps tight. "But they will help you get a better grip on smooth surfaces. Ready?"

I shrugged helplessly. "As I'll ever be."

Janice nodded. "Right. Let's go."

With that, she launched herself over the side of the balustrade. I gasped, leaning over to see her clambering effortlessly down the side of the concrete tower. In two seconds flat she was on the ground, unharmed and undaunted. So that was how Joanie had done it.

"You'll be fine, Laura," Shailene said next to me. "Just do what she did. I'll watch to make sure you don't fall."

I exhaled shakily. "Promise?"

"Promise," she said.

I swallowed hard, swung my leg over the balustrade, and let go. My stomach dropped out from under me as I fell for just an instant, but then my hand shot out, and though there were no handholds to cling to, it stuck to the surface and held me. My heart pounded in my ears, but when I didn't plummet to my doom, it eased slightly. I reached down, like for an invisible ladder rung, and stuck again. The gloves were like magnets, holding me to the tower's surface.

"See, you're doing great," Shailene said, shimmying down beside me. "Now let's go. There's no time to waste."

Like that, we were off. I cut my conscious mind off, forbidding it to think about how impossible this was, or how dangerous. I refused to allow myself to think that I should go slowly, hesitantly. There was no time for caution.

I landed hard on my boots and kept running, racing to keep pace with Janice and Shailene. The scenery around us blurred together in a whirl of colors as we ran ever faster. My eyes had to struggle to keep up with the rapidly-changing street before me, and my mind strained to keep a grip on Andronicus' signal now that the amplifier was no longer boosting my psychic range.

"We have to hurry," I called. "He won't be there long. I can feel it."

"We'll need to catch a ride," Janice said, veering left.

"What?" I asked, but within an instant I had my answer. The air around us vibrated with the rumble of an approaching train.

"We're close to the entrance of the Tube," Shailene said, looking at me over her shoulder as we ran. I struggled to keep up with her—she and Janice were in much better shape than I was, what with their two-hundred jumping jacks a day, or whatever it is cheerleaders do to keep in shape. "The speed picks up as soon as soon as the trains can get underground. If we can catch this one before it enters the tunnel, we'll be at Union Station in just a few minutes."

"The Tube?" I repeated, blanching. That was the underground stretch of the PeRT system, cutting under the hills of the City, and even part of the Bay itself. I always got claustrophobic in those parts of my commute. "Isn't that a bit snug?"

"We'll fit," Janice said confidently. She slowed as we reached the end of the road, where a heavily-graffitied wall and a *Do Not Enter* sign marked the edge of the tracks. She perched on the balls of her feet, craning her head to see down the line. "Get ready. The train's coming."

"And what do we do when it comes?" I asked.

"Jump. And hold on."

"Seriously? That's the plan?" I squeaked.

"You'll be fine," she said. "All right, on the count of three."

The train was bearing down the track at what seemed an impossible speed, even though I'd just been running almost that fast myself. It began to accelerate as it approached the entrance to the Tube. How the hell was I supposed to launch myself at a moving train and not get myself killed?

"One..."

Think of old school freight-hoppers, Laura. They could do it. It must not be that impossible.

"Two..."

Yeah, but how fast were those freight trains going when people hopped on them? Probably not this fast.

"Three..."

But you're not an ordinary human, Laura.

"Go!"

Shailene and Janice jumped effortlessly, and I followed a fraction of a second after them. If I'd been moving in fast-forward before, now I felt like I was moving in slow-mo, reacting too slowly, moving too slowly. I saw Shailene easily grab the side of the moving train, but I stumbled, slipping and nearly losing my grip on the speeding metal. I grabbed frantically, trying to get purchase on anything. This was it. I'd screwed up, and now it was over. I'd slip right off the side of the moving train, crushed to death under its wheels like that Anesidoran sentry I'd shoved on the tracks.

"Laura!" Shailene shouted.

Strong hands grabbed the back of my shirt, dragging me up the side of the train. Janice. I grasped frantically, gripping her arm. Between the two of us, I managed to scramble up onto the roof just as the train sped into the darkness of the Tube.

I ducked my head, feeling the ceiling too close to my head as the train zoomed through the dark. Neon lights in rainbow colors streaked past, blurring together—red, blue, green, purple. A novel effect for the people inside the train, but out here it just added to my anxiety, my awareness that I was traveling way too fast in a space that was way too small.

"You did it," Shailene said. She started to reach to pat my shoulder, but then she hesitated and gave me a thumbs-up instead.

"Yeah," I managed to reply after a moment.

"Don't relax yet," said Janice. In the dark, I could only see her silhouette, outlined by the neon lights. "We're coming up to Union Station in just a couple minutes. Stay focused. Don't lose sight of our objective. We need to be able to find him."

"Right. Focus," I said, more to myself than as a response. I could feel us drawing closer to him. I tried not to think how the swirling colors of the lights inside the tube reminded me of his oscillating skin in my nightmare.

The train sped through the dark.

- Chapter 9 -

Every fiber in me felt alert as the train pulled into Union Station. Even the hairs on my arms seemed to stand on end. I wasn't sure if Andronicus could sense me like I could sense him, but I undeniably felt like I was being watched.

"Do you feel him, Laura?" Janice asked in a low voice as the train passengers started to disembark.

I closed my eyes and grimaced. "I do, but... I'm not sure where he's at. Everything feels too loud all of a sudden. It's like he's everywhere, and I can't focus."

"That means he's nearby," Janice said. "The ability to sense isn't like GPS. It's far less precise. It's more like trying to see through binoculars—when you're far away, it makes distant objects look close; but when you're too close, everything becomes blurry."

I nodded. That was exactly how it felt. Snatches of color and shape, the idea of what I should be able to see, but trying to make that picture out just made me nauseous.

"We should fan out," Shailene said. "Search the whole station before he disappears."

"I don't think we should split up," I replied. "What with everything that's been going on. Isolating yourself seems like the best way for them to get you."

"Laura's right," Janice said. "We stay together. Try to look casual, like we're just three travelers."

"Oh, that'll be easy to pull off. Three travelers who rode in on the roof of a train," I said.

Janice rolled her eyes and adjusted the straps of her backpack. "Just come on."

"But how do we keep people from seeing us?" I asked, glancing hesitantly down at the train platform below us. I knew we needed to get moving before the train took off again, but I was nervous.

Shailene nudged my shoulder. "Does it make sense for three women in workout gear—well, two in workout gear, one in, uh, that"—she gestured to my mostly-leather alien-hunter ensemble—"to be on the roof of a train? Or to be moving as fast as we do, or to be fighting giant insectoids?"

"Of course not," I said.

"That's how we're not seen. The human brain can't process things that don't make sense to it. So they look past us, not at us."

"If you say so." I watched as Janice smiled briskly and jumped down into the throngs of people. No one seemed to notice her, or Shailene as she followed. So, reluctantly, I leapt down onto the platform (and landed neatly, not even rolling my ankle in those boots, if I do say so myself).

Union Station was the largest PeRT stop in the City, even bigger than San Luis. Different lines wove together in an intricate puzzle, switching and dumping trains at a dozen different platforms on the south side of the building. On the north side, the Amtrak line ran on separate tracks, bringing people from other parts of the state and beyond. The crowds were thick here, especially at this time of day. Tourists finishing up their spring breaks were hurrying to get back home; students on their way back to school were piling off the shuttle from the airport and scurrying to get to the right platform before their train left the station. As impossible as it seemed, no one did notice us. We were just three faces in the immense crowd.

I just wished that I could sense better. Now that I'd figured this ability out, it already felt disorienting for it to not be working. I realized I must have been aware of it subconsciously for a long time and never paid any attention to it. When I'd feel uneasy in crowds in the past, did that mean he'd been there? Or maybe it wasn't just limited to him. Maybe I could sense other Anesidorans, too, and I'd just never realized it.

We scoped out the bottom level, trains coming in and out of the tube, to no avail before moving to the upper level. Here, the lines that ran over the top of the tube and into the foothills intersected. A band of red glass in the roof let light filter through, casting a pinkish haze over everyone standing beneath it on the platform.

"Nothing," Shailene said, looking around. "I don't see or sense anyone. What about you, Laura?"

I shook my head. "Maybe I was wrong about him being here, specifically."

"Or maybe they know we're onto them," Janice said. "We might need to disappear for a bit."

"Those antennas Shailene used before?" I suggested.

"Yes. And the amplifier couldn't hurt either," Janice agreed. She led Shailene and me over to a bench near the rear platform. I sat beside her, watching as she slung her backpack around to her front. "It's important that we stay quiet while this is running. It scrambles the sentries' vision sensors, but they can still—"

I didn't hear what she said next. As she pulled the tripod setup out of her backpack, a manila folder slipped forward. My eye caught on the neatly-typed label on its tab: *Philip Gregg.*

I only saw it for a second before she zipped the backpack shut again, but it made my heart completely stop for a couple of beats. Janice had called my dad "Gregg" before. I'd thought she'd said "Greg," like the first name; but seeing it together with "Philip" like that... Did that folder have something to do with my dad?

And, if so, why did Janice have it in her backpack?

The three of us sat silently for several minutes, my mind reeling, trying to think of a way to get Janice's backpack away from her. I had to see what was in that file folder. But how was I supposed to get it without her noticing me?

She glanced at me, like she knew what I was thinking. "Laura," she whispered, "do you sense anything?"

It took me a minute to realize what she meant. I tore my thoughts away from the backpack and the folder inside. "O-Oh," I stammered once my brain had caught up with me. "Not any more than I—"

"Look," Shailene hissed, cutting me off. I turned in the direction she was pointing. Standing in front of Platform C, flanked on either side by sentries, was Erikka. It was like she'd materialized out of thin air; one second she hadn't been there, the next second she was.

"Erikka!" Shailene cried, jumping to her feet.

I gasped and lunged forward, reaching across Janice before she could react and grabbing Shailene by the shirttail. "Wait!"

"What do you mean, 'wait'? We have to move fast, get her away from those sentries before the train comes in."

"Look at her, Shailene," I said in a hoarse whisper. "Those sentries aren't restraining her. Remember what I said? After Andronicus hit her with that red lightning, she went with him voluntarily. And now she's standing there, again, voluntarily." I looked Shailene in the eyes imploringly. "He's doing something to their minds. If we reveal ourselves to her, I don't think she'll come with us willingly."

Shailene looked like she was about to argue, but Janice broke in, her voice low. "And if we give ourselves away now, we'll lose what could be our last chance to find out where they're going and see if the other girls are there."

"So what are we supposed to do, just let her go?" Shailene snapped.

"We'll watch," said Janice. "And see if we can figure out their destination when we see what train they board."

A beep sounded over the loudspeakers, indicating that a train was arriving. "And now's our chance. Here it comes,"

I said.

But the words died in my throat when the rumbling line of cars appeared, slowing to a halt next to Platform C. The L.E.D. display on the front car was blank, unlit. The same thing for the sign over the platform itself. No destination.

"Are you kidding me?" I groaned. "Not even a number! How are we supposed to track a blank train?"

"Come on." Shailene leapt to her feet. "We can't let it get away."

Erikka and the sentries were boarding, the pneumatic doors swishing shut behind them. "Shailene, hold on!" Janice cried, racing after her. But it didn't matter—the train was already pulling away from the platform. So much for a twenty-second loading time.

"We can still catch it up," Shailene said, starting to break into a run.

Janice grabbed her arm, pulling her back. "No! It's too dangerous."

"But, Coach!"

"Maybe someone knows where it's going," I suggested. I glanced around, noticing a guy who looked close to my age wearing a polo shirt with the PeRT logo embroidered on the lapel, sweeping litter into a dustbin. I hurried over to him. "Excuse me, where is the train that just left Platform C heading?"

He looked at me blankly. "How should I know? Check the sign."

Coming up beside me, Shailene gritted her teeth. "No kidding. That train wasn't listed on the sign. And it didn't have a destination marked on the train itself, either."

"Oh." He flashed us a devious grin, like he was about to share a juicy secret. "That must have been one of the ghost trains, then."

I blinked incredulously. "I'm sorry, *ghost train?*"

"Yeah, they're trains that don't take passengers, but they're legally mandated to stay in operation, even though they run empty."

Janice folded her arms, quirking an eyebrow. "Why would the law require that?"

"Don't ask me. I don't run this place. I just work here." He propped his broom against the wall and looked at us a bit more seriously. "I heard it was some kind of bureaucratic thing, like they need trains to run on certain lines in order to keep the lines open. Probably if they want to expand the commuter system in the future or something. It's cheaper to maintain an existing line than to build a new one, or repair it after it's been closed."

Janice nodded thoughtfully. "Okay. Thanks for your

help."

We moved away from him, back to the corner where we'd been sitting before.

"So what does that mean?" I asked.

"I'm not sure. It could mean that the Anesidorans are taking advantage of these ghost trains to get where they need to go." Janice turned back to face Platform C, adjusting the straps on her backpack. I tried not to stare as she did so. Now was not the time to get distracted, even if I was still dying to know about the contents of that folder. "But it also means that we can't bank on another train heading the same way today. We'll have to catch it up."

"Finally, some sense," Shailene muttered under her breath.

"Laura," said Janice, "can you still feel Andronicus nearby?"

I closed my eyes, focusing. "No... Wait. I do feel something." It was *like* him, but different. I couldn't put my finger on it, but I knew I had felt it before. "Moving eastbound. Or possibly northeast?"

"Got it. Let's move. If we hurry, we can reconnect with that ghost train before it splits from the main lines." She quickly shut down the cloaking system, shoving the two tripods into her backpack and slinging it back around her shoulder. "Ready?"

A train was pulling away from Platform B. Janice broke into a run, coming up alongside it, Shailene and I close behind. I didn't give myself a second to be nervous. Not this time. I just jumped, letting my instincts take over.

And this time, I didn't fall.

"Good job, Laura," Shailene said, grinning at me as we scrambled up onto the roof. "But don't relax yet. We're going to have to move if we want to catch up with that other train."

The fierce wind whipped my hair around, tossing wisps of it into my mouth and then ripping them free again.

"Laura, can you still feel him?" Janice shouted. I could barely hear her over the wind. "Are they still traveling in this direction?"

I strained to concentrate. "No. They're starting to veer more north."

"Right. Time to switch lines. There's a crossing in half a mile. Get ready."

We jumped from train to train, the sun burning hot and bright overhead, the wind stinging my face. I could feel that we were getting closer to whomever I was sensing; but the nearer we got, the more certain I was that it wasn't Andronicus.

We were deep in the foothills now, the tracks winding

their way through narrow valleys and high, rounded bluffs. Sheep and cows grazed in the grass, still green from the winter rains but beginning to turn the familiar yellow of the rest of the year. The trees were more sparse here, but patches of oaks growing alongside the tracks made visibility difficult.

"We're getting close," I shouted, the wind snatching my voice away as soon as the words had left my mouth. "As soon as we get around this corner, we should be able to see the other train."

We wound around a rocky headland and then the hills opened up into a wide valley. A few hundred feet above us, I could see the interstate, loaded with cars, and beyond that, a hillside dotted with dozens of wind turbines. I craned my head to see the ghost train on the far north edge of the valley. The place where the tracks diverged. Our train wouldn't get any closer than it was now; how were we supposed to catch it up?

"There they are—"

"Get down!"

The words tore from my mouth before my brain could even process why. I hurled myself down on the roof of the train, Janice and Shailene beside me, and half a second later, something whizzed above my head, exploding into the branches of the trees behind us with a deafening crack.

Before I could react, there was a thud, and I looked up from my prone position to see two sentries and a man in a hooded jacket standing on the car in front of us.

My stomach knotted inside me. This was who I'd sensed earlier. But who was he? He was taller than Andronicus, more lithely built. Something about his stance made him seem younger. Though his face was concealed by the hood, he still felt familiar to me.

"This ends now," he said. He clenched his fist, revealing a set of brass knuckles with spikes on them, like some kind of Wolverine wannabe.

"I don't think so," growled Shailene, lunging for him.

I gasped—engaging a man who was wearing spiked knuckles in hand-to-hand combat didn't exactly seem like the smartest plan of action—but one of the two sentries intercepted her, drawing her away from the hooded man. Janice whirled neatly into Shailene's place, lashing out with her foot and connecting directly with her sternum. "Stay back, Laura," she ordered.

I watched, dumbfounded, as the hooded man swung his fist at Janice. She ducked, but the spikes on his knuckles dragged across her shoulder, severing the strap of her backpack. She cried out in pain, clutching at her shoulder as the bag fell, ricocheting off the top of the train. Without thinking, I dove for it, catching it just before it fell off the roof. Quickly, I unzipped it, starting to rummage through it. There had to be some weapons in here, something I could use…

"Laura Clark."

My head snapped up. One of the sentries was looming over me, its arms like lobster claws. I realized in horror that it had been talking to me. How did it know my name?

"You are in violation of Statute 127.8," it said, its mandibles tremoring. "Stand down immediately, or I shall have to take you into custody."

"You're not taking me anywhere, cockroach," I spat, lunging forward and swinging blindly at it with my fist.

The sentry dodged my punch easily. "Andronicus shall hear of this," it said, grabbing my upper arm with its claws and squeezing painfully. It was strong, and I realized that I had been a moron to try to confront it when I had no clue how to fight. Janice had been right; I should have stayed back.

I struggled violently. "Let go of me," I growled, wrenching my arm against the sentry's iron grip. *Come on, Laura, use those superpowers,* I thought desperately. *You know you've got them…* My mind raced as the air whipped past me, grasping for anything, any kind of hidden strength my body might be concealing from me that I could use against him.

My skin suddenly burned in the spot on my arm the sentry was clutching. There was a sharp, razor-like pain, and then my arm started to morph. The skin rippled, oscillating a prism of colors before turning black, hardening.

Looking very much like the arm of the sentry itself.

I screamed, ripping my arm away with a strength I didn't know I had. My skin bubbled, shimmering as my arm reformed itself into its regular shape. The sentry staggered back in what I thought was surprise at my sudden transformation—but then I heard Shailene shout, "Laura, get down!"

I ducked just as Shailene pummeled the sentry a second time with some kind of nightstick that crackled with electricity. The sentry reeled, spinning away from me and turning its attention to Shailene, struggling to maintain its balance as toxic electricity rippled through its body.

Blue light pulsed across the weapon's surface, sparking as she brandished it like a sword.

Before she could swing again, the second sentry charged her. The two of them thrusted and parried, electric nightstick to claw. The first sentry shook itself off, recovering from the electric attack, and jumped into the melee.

I ripped the backpack open again, rummaging through it for any kind of weapon I could find. There was nothing recognizable as a weapon in the bag, though, nothing like a gun or Taser or even a nightstick like Shailene's. I settled for one of the cloaking tripods.

"Hey, Lobster Face," I yelled, rushing forward. "Two against one isn't fair play!" I bashed the first sentry over the head as hard as I could with the tripod. This didn't have much effect, but it distracted the creature long enough for Shailene to get the upper hand again. Electricity pulsed as she slammed the nightstick into the sentry's chest. It screamed, a horrible, grating sound, collapsing to its knees. I raised my arm, preparing to club it with the tripod again.

"Laura Clark," a girl's voice said.

I froze, suddenly rooted in my spot, my arm awkwardly fixed over my head like a statue.

Everything seemed to stand still, the train almost feeling like it was moving in slow motion. Even my heart seemed to stop as I saw her approaching Shailene and me across the roof of the rear car. The wind from the fast-moving train whipped her braids around her face. Behind her, I could see Janice frozen three cars ahead of us, seemingly rooted in place the way I felt now. The man in the hood stood beside her, not touching her, not holding her in her spot—just watching her. We all were riveted, staring at the girl approaching as casually as if she were walking down the street and not the roof of a speeding train.

Erikka.

"That is enough out of you," she said to me, her expression stern. She didn't seem any different than when I'd seen her this morning—no glowing eyes, no visible signs that she'd been possessed. But her entire demeanor was changed. When she spoke, she almost sounded like a female version of Andronicus, cool and smooth. "This is your final warning. Stay out of Anesidoran affairs, or there will be consequences."

I was trembling, but I still couldn't move. My ears rang from the stabbing pain in my head, centered between my eyes.

She smiled, a slight quirk to the corners of her lips. "That's more like it. And as for you—" She turned to Shailene, who was frozen in a crouch, staring at Erikka unblinkingly. Erikka lifted her hand, beckoning to her. "It's time for this to end."

She was going to erase Shailene, as surely as Andronicus had erased her. "No," I tried to say, but my voice caught in my throat, and the word came out like a croak. It was like being trapped in a dream where you can see what's happening but can't move your limbs, can't get the words to come out.

Shailene rose, taking a step forward.

This couldn't happen.

Her expression was blank as she stared at Erikka, her eyes glassy. My head pounded. It was this morning all over again. The red lightning would flash, and then Shailene would be gone. They'd all be gone. And only I would know what had happened.

I couldn't let it happen.

Erikka reached for Shailene, and I hurled myself forward. My head felt like it was going to explode as I charged ahead, somehow breaking the inertia of the spell. Lights flashed in my vision—not the red lightning, but the sparking fireworks of the headache ripping through me. I couldn't see where I was going, but I felt my body collide with another. I didn't know whose. We toppled backward, and then there was nothing beneath my feet. Nothing but air.

The nothingness only lasted a second, and then we slammed into the ground with an agonizing thud. I felt myself disentangle from whomever I'd tackled, and I rolled and bumped painfully across rocks and dirt. Tears stung at my eyes from the pain, and I knew that if I had been an ordinary human, I'd be dead.

After a moment, I managed to force my eyes open and found myself collapsed in a pile of broken branches. My jeans were shredded, blood beginning to pool from scrapes and roadburns on my knees. I could feel bruises forming all over my body, but incredibly, it didn't feel like anything was broken.

I struggled into a sitting position. Crumpled on the ground five feet away from me was Shailene.

"Shailene!" I gasped, crawling painfully over to her. I started to reach out to her, but she was already stirring.

"What happened?" she asked weakly.

"Don't you remember?" I asked her.

She blinked at me, like she was struggling to remember my face. Then recognition dawned. "No," she said. "The last thing I remember is the sentry grabbing you. Then it's like... it's like waking up from a dream. I can almost see it, but it's slipping away."

"It was Erikka," I said.

"What?" Shailene hissed.

"She tried to... She tried to do to you whatever Andronicus did to her. It's like I said earlier: The Anesidorans must be brainwashing the Strikers. It's the only thing that makes sense."

"How did we get away?"

"I, uh... I guess I pushed you off the train." I hesitated. "You're still you, right? You don't feel a sudden urge to go join with the Anesidorans?"

"Of course not," she said.

I sighed in relief. "Good. I stopped her in time."

Shailene breathed out, looking down, a slight tinge of pink on her dirt-encrusted cheeks. "Thank you," she whispered. She sat up, pulling at her hair, brushing it away from her neck. She looked around. "Where's Coach?"

"Oh," I said, my eyes widening. The force of the impact had knocked my senses out of me. I had forgotten Janice completely. "She's—" I looked down the track, but the train was long gone. The valley was empty apart from the freeway above our heads. Janice was nowhere to be seen. "I don't know."

"What?!" Shailene jumped up so fast I could barely see her movement. She started forward, but her knees gave out and she pitched forward. "We have to follow them! We have to save her!"

"Maybe she's okay," I said, limping over to her. "Maybe she got off farther up the line and she'll backtrack."

"No," Shailene said, a note of hysteria in her voice. "I can't feel her anymore, Laura."

"What?" I closed my eyes, trying to reach out for Janice myself, but there was nothing.

"She's gone." Shailene's voice broke. "Janice is gone. They have her. She's gone."

"Shailene, it's okay. We can still—"

She shook her head, curling into herself. Sobs racked her. I wanted to reach out to her, wrap my arms around her, do something comforting, but I was afraid to touch her. I didn't know what would happen, and I didn't dare incapacitate myself or her.

I looked around, feeling helpless. On the ground, several yards from where we'd landed, Janice's backpack lay in a heap. I'd thought my answers might be in that bag. Maybe they still were. I'd seen the amplifier, her phone and tablet, and a bunch of tech that I didn't recognize when I'd been looking for a weapon. If they hadn't broken in the fall, we could try to use them. Maybe it wasn't too late.

"We'll find her, Shailene," I said weakly.

She shook her head again, and I watched her as she cried.

- Chapter 10 -

Shailene and I walked back to Union Station in silence. The train we'd been following had disappeared, and after the fight, I couldn't sense the hooded man or Andronicus anywhere. Going back to the station and waiting for the next ghost train seemed like our only choice.

As we meandered alongside the tracks, I rolled up my sleeves, letting the sun hit my skin as much as I could. Beside me, Shailene had taken off her jacket, tying its arms around her waist. By the time we were approaching the City limits, the bloody scabs on my knees and elbows had already shrunk and begun to fade, the sun's rays accelerating the healing process.

"So, I guess that's a thing that happens now," I commented, looking myself over. I wondered when it had started. Had I always been this way, and just never noticed?

I couldn't remember ever cutting myself up this badly before, so maybe that was why. Not that you could tell now. My ripped jeans and dirty knees made me look grungy, but that was preferable to looking like I'd been in a car accident.

"If you're going to build a super army, you want to make sure they heal quickly," Shailene said dourly. She looked down at her phone again. She'd been trying to get a signal as we'd been walking, eager to get a hold of the other cheerleaders—what was left of them, anyway. She told me as we trudged down the track that as of this morning, it had just been her, Janice and Erikka, one sophomore, and a couple freshmen left, out of their typical squad of twelve. They'd already lost two since this morning, and if I hadn't body-slammed her, Shailene would be gone, too. I dreaded to think what had happened to the other girls while we'd been separated.

She held her phone up, shading it from the sun with her hand and peering at the dim screen. A spiderweb of cracks ran through it; the impact of our bodies hitting the ground had shattered both our phones, though Shailene's had gotten the brunt of it. Mine just had a single fracture—enough to be annoying, but not enough to prevent me from using it as normal. Shailene would be lucky if she could place outgoing calls from hers.

"Two bars," she said. "I'm going to give it a try."

She dialed a number and held the phone up to her ear. No one answered. She tried this five more times. By the time she hung up the last time, she was white as a sheet, though I could see she was trying to keep the strain from showing on her face.

"No one," she said.

"Maybe the signal's not strong enough to get through. Or maybe your phone is too smashed and it's not actually working," I suggested. "Do you want to try mine?"

"No. It's working. I... I can't feel any of them, Laura."

Her voice was hollow. I tried to suppress the panic that the numbness of her tone made me feel. "You don't think...?"

"I don't see how there's anything else *to* think."

"Then that means... you're the last one."

She didn't respond. The silence was agonizing.

"It's okay. It'll be okay," I said at last, not sure if I was trying more to reassure Shailene or myself. "We'll find them. At least we know now that you not being able to sense them doesn't mean they're"—I swallowed—"you know, dead."

She nodded. "The Anesidorans are doing something to them. I don't know what. But there still has to be a chance we can get them back." She clenched her fist. "There has to be."

"What about the I.G.A.?" I asked. "Shouldn't you call them? Bring them in on it?"

Shailene snorted. "Screw the I.G.A. They're worse than useless."

My eyes widened. "Whoa, what now?"

"You think we didn't alert them as soon as this started happening? They're a bunch of idiots. More than that... they're shady. Remember what your dad said? I'm starting to think he was right."

I shifted awkwardly, remembering the folder in Janice's backpack. I'd glanced inside the bag before we'd started heading back to make sure it was still there, but I hadn't been able to look at it yet. I opened my mouth to tell Shailene about it, but something made me hold back. Maybe I was wrong. Maybe it had nothing to do with my dad.

Or worse, maybe it did.

Regardless, for some reason I didn't want Shailene around when I looked at that folder. Not until I knew what was really inside it. So I shut my mouth, and we trudged on in silence.

When we drew close to the station, I hesitated. "Maybe

let's not go back in there yet," I said. "I don't sense Andronicus or his hoodie sidekick around, but they're probably looking for you." I looked over at the tall clock tower on the Hilltop Mall. "We can go in there, get cleaned up, get something to eat... regroup. Figure out what we're going to do next, rather than just barreling in."

She followed my gaze up to the clock tower. It was just after three o'clock. My stomach was growling—I hadn't had anything but those granola bars and yogurt since breakfast this morning, eight hours ago at that point. Shailene hadn't even had that much. She was probably starving.

"Okay," she said after a moment. Together, we crossed the bustling street.

The Hilltop Mall wasn't an ordinary shopping mall. For one thing, it was almost as old as the City itself. The three-story shopping center had been built in the late eighteen-hundreds—it was one of the few buildings in the City that had been out of the path of the Great Fire a century ago—and it was rare in that it had been built *as* a shopping center, rather than being converted from another type of building. That made it one of the oldest original malls on the West Coast, and it also made it incredibly unique. Unlike other shopping plazas with their bright lights, linoleum floors and wide, open floor plans, the Hilltop was a maze of hardwood floors and winding corridors. The food court area was the only space in the mall that opened up to all three floors of the building. Clusters of small, old-fashioned tables wound their way between food carts on the ground floor, while balconies on the second and third floors led to more traditional restaurants: Sol Azteca Mexican Food, Papadopoulos' Greek Cuisine, Genovese Italian Delicatessen and Bakery.

"What are you thinking you might want?" I asked, gesturing to the signs hanging from the wrought iron railings above us.

"I don't know." Shailene sank into an empty chair next to the Dolce Mamma ice cream cart. I took the seat across from her, setting Janice's backpack on the floor between my feet and glancing around at the crowded food court to make sure there weren't any sentries around. "I don't know if I can eat. I feel like everything is just starting to catch up with me." She slumped onto the table, crossing her arms and burying her face in her elbows. "How the hell am I supposed to do this alone? What am I supposed to do without Janice?" Her voice was muffled by her arms, but it sounded like it was about to break.

I watched her fretfully, thinking back to the way she'd collapsed when she'd learned that we'd lost Janice. She'd been angry and upset about the disappearance of the other cheerleaders, but that had been nothing compared to the way she'd sobbed when I'd said Janice was gone. I hadn't thought it was possible for cool, unflappable Shailene to lose it like that.

"You're really close with Janice, huh?" I asked tentatively. She didn't respond. Awkwardly, I added, "I mean, that's natural. She's your coach, and your squad isn't exactly normal. You probably have a tighter bond than most—"

"She's my mom."

I broke off midsentence, my mouth hanging open like a fish. "What?"

She kept her head on the table, but she looked up at me over her folded arms, her black hair pooling around her like some kind of undersea creature surfacing from the water. "You heard me."

"Oh," I stammered. "I'm sorry. I didn't realize—that is, you don't look alike, and you always call her by her first name, or Coach—"

"I'm adopted," Shailene said. "It was kind of recent. I mean..." She sighed, sitting up and shifting in her chair, not looking at me even though she spoke to me. "I lived with my birth parents until right before I started high school. But things weren't... good. They hadn't been for a while.

Not since they found out about me liking girls."

Her voice was strained, and she rubbed the back of her neck compulsively. It looked like just a nervous gesture, but now that I'd seen her tattoo, I knew it was likely more than that.

"Shailene," I said, "you don't have to—"

She shook her head, still not looking at me. "No. It's okay. I need to tell someone. And… I trust you, I guess." I thought I saw the faintest tinge of pink on her cheeks, but then she tossed her hair and her features disappeared behind the curtain of dark curls. "Anyway, things weren't good with my birth parents. But they got a lot worse after I was abducted. When I disappeared, they thought I'd run away. Janice was the one who brought me back after the I.G.A. rescued me. She tried to explain what had happened, explain that I was going to need supervision because of the powers I might have now. They didn't believe her. They thought it was drugs, or gangs, or even demons from Hell—they'd believe anything but the truth. And whatever they believed, they believed most of all that it was my own fault. For being the way I am."

Hot tears stung at my eyes. I blinked them away. I wanted to say something, anything, but the words got stuck in my throat. My parents had never been anything but supportive of me. No one in my family had ever been anything but accepting of me—not even Lola, as much as she teased. I couldn't imagine what it must have been like for Shailene.

"I don't remember much about it," she went on. "The whole time around my abduction is fuzzy. I... I talked to a therapist about it in high school. Someone with the I.G.A. who worked with rescues. She said it's normal to block out pieces of traumatic events." She shrugged one shoulder. "I don't know. I just remember that right before the abduction, I'd been in trouble for kissing a girl. I don't even remember anything about her, really. I don't remember it happening so much as I remember my parents *talking* about it happening—yelling at me about it. But when Janice brought me back after the abduction, my parents said it was a sign. That I was *'touched by the Devil'*. They tried to hurt me," she said, the numbness in her voice making me wince. "But Janice intervened. She let me stay with her. In my darkest time, she was there for me. She kept me safe. We changed my name; I couldn't take Janice's last name because my parents knew that, so I took Peterson, which is Janice's mom's maiden name. And Shailene..." Her eyes clouded, and she looked down, seeming far away for a minute. "Shailene is a name I chose for myself."

"Shailene is a pretty name," I said, not knowing what

else to say. "It suits you." As the sentence left my mouth, I felt a strange sensation—like I'd said those words before. But when I tried to think about it, there was the headache again.

Damn this. Damn whatever it was.

I stretched my hand out, stopping myself an inch away from her bare arms. I didn't want to touch her for fear of bringing that stabbing pain back, but I wanted to be close to her. I wanted her to not feel alone.

She turned her head, looking at my fingers trailing a hair's breadth from her pale skin and smiling. I smiled back.

"I feel like chips and salsa," she said, her voice thick and husky from the tears. "What about you?"

"I think I'll get a bowl of pho." I gestured to one of the carts across from us on the ground floor.

She nodded and stood, brushing her hair back with one hand. Just like that a mask seemed to fall over her, that smooth veneer of unflappability. But I'd seen what lay beneath it now. It made me feel protective of her.

As Shailene made for the stairs, I pretended to fidget in my pockets for my wallet. But as soon as she was out of sight, I reached under the table and pulled out Janice's backpack.

The manila folder was crumpled from the way the backpack had been tossed around, but I smoothed it, looking again at the name on the tab. *Philip Gregg.* I hesitated for a long moment, afraid of what I might find inside. I couldn't quite bring myself to open it. But if I just sat here staring at it, Shailene would come back and I'd have to explain myself. So I took a deep breath and opened the folder.

It was some kind of transcript. It looked like it had been typed on an old-school typewriter, and the paper was yellowed at the edges. The official I.G.A. emblem (the real one that said *Galactic* on it) was on the letterhead, and it was dated a little over twenty years ago. I flipped through the pages, my eyes crossing. I didn't understand what any of this meant, and I needed to figure it out before Shailene came back. It appeared to be an interview between an internal affairs investigator and this Philip Gregg guy about an incident that had occurred in June the year before the interview. From what I could glean, Philip Gregg and his partner had been on a mission to intercept a "subject of interest." Whatever that meant. The way they were talking, I couldn't tell if they meant an Anesidoran or an abductee.

Maybe both, I thought with a shudder. Was it someone that the I.G.A. hadn't been able to rescue? Shailene had said that they weren't able to save everyone. What happened to the people that the Anesidorans managed to keep? I hadn't thought about it that much until now, but she kept saying they were trying to build an army—one that could infiltrate Earth. What if abductees were all around us, just waiting for the right moment to kill us all in our sleep? My skin crawled at the thought.

Whatever had happened twenty years ago, it hadn't gone well for Philip Gregg and his partner. The "subject of interest" caught onto them and attacked. Philip was injured—but his partner had died.

I chewed on the inside of my cheek as I read the words over and over. Was this my dad? Is that why he'd gotten a dispensation from the I.G.A.? How could he have kept this secret for all these years?

In my pocket, my phone buzzed, the digital chimes of my text tone practically giving me a heart attack. I fought to catch my breath; then, glancing around to make sure Shailene was still out of sight, I shoved the folder back in Janice's backpack and the backpack under the table again. Then I pulled my phone out.

It's ok if you're busy. Just let me know, ok?

Shit. Ana. She'd wanted to know if I'd go to dinner with her and Damien tonight. I hadn't answered earlier. Guilt washed over me. I didn't want her to think I was snubbing her because of her boyfriend. But I also didn't really want to have dinner with Damien, either. Especially when Shailene was so upset about Janice. And I also didn't like the thought of leaving Shailene alone, not when the Anesidorans were apparently gunning for all the Bayview cheerleaders.

My thumb hovered over the reply screen. I didn't know how to respond. Maybe I could talk her into coming with us. Not like that would be super awkward or anything. My big, her boyfriend, and the gorgeous superhuman brunette that I may or may not have been developing an enormous crush on. It would be like the world's most uncomfortable double not-date.

"Didn't you get any food?"

I jumped twenty-seven feet in the air at the sound of Shailene's voice. She stood over me holding a plastic tray with a steaming hot enchilada and a guacamole tostada on it. Hurriedly, I shoved my phone back in my pocket. "No, not yet. I got distracted checking my messages," I said. "Here, you hold the table for us. I'll go get my soup now."

Five minutes later, I was back at the table with a heaping bowl of pho and a side order of spring rolls. I watched Shailene as she dunked a tortilla chip in the Styrofoam container of salsa she'd gotten from Sol Azteca and popped it into her mouth with a crunch, seemingly lost in thought.

"The question is," she said after swallowing, "if we find another ghost train, how do we get aboard without the

Anesidorans stopping us again?"

I shoveled in a mouthful of noodles. Apparently, she wasn't planning on stopping for the day. Dinner with Ana and Damien was out, then. "Maybe we can sneak on board," I said. "The cloaking device is out, though. I lost one of the tripods when we fell."

She shrugged. "It's just as well. That's not always effective, and it wouldn't work when we're moving, so we'd still have to find a way to get on board without them spotting us. They're going to be on the alert after what happened earlier."

I sighed, resting my cheek on my hand. "If only there was a way we could hide in plain sight..." I started, then trailed off. My hand. I sat upright again, looking at the lines on my palm. I'd almost forgotten about what had happened when the sentry'd had a hold of me, how my skin had rippled and changed. "Shailene, is one of the abilities we have... shape-shifting?"

"Not that I know of. Why?"

I hesitated, not sure if I should say anything to her about it. But she'd been so candid with me to this point. I couldn't keep hiding things from her. "Well," I said slowly, "something weird happened to me earlier." I told her about what had happened on the train.

Shailene stared at me, one of her perfect eyebrows arched. "That's... different," she said. I flushed, and she added hurriedly, "No, but it's good. Your powers are different from the ones I've seen, Laura, but that doesn't mean it's anything unusual. Janice might have known more. Regardless"—she chewed the corner of her lip thoughtfully—"that would work in our favor. Do you think you can maintain it if you're not touching the person... or thing, in the sentries' case... whose form you're taking?"

"I don't know. I kind of freaked out when it happened," I admitted. "I'd have to try it again."

She nodded, looking around the food court with a new spark of light in her eyes. I smiled involuntarily. For the first time since this morning, she seemed to be back to her old self. "Well, not here. There're too many people around. Come on. There's a single-stall bathroom behind the hair salon on the second floor. We can do it in there."

My face flushed and I looked down, trying to suppress the feelings that sentence stirred up inside me. *We aren't going to the bathroom to make out*, I reminded myself, my cheeks hot. We had work to do.

Still, I couldn't help the butterflies that swirled around my stomach as I grabbed Janice's backpack from under the table and hurried toward the stairs after Shailene.

- Chapter 11 -

It wasn't until we got into the bathroom that I realized the major flaw in our plan.

"Um, how are we supposed to do this, exactly?" I asked. "Since, you know, we can't…"

"Oh," Shailene said, her face as red as mine felt. "Good point. Well…" She looked around the small space desperately, as if the tile walls would give her some kind of idea. Once again, I thought glumly about what a travesty of justice this was. Her skin looked so soft and perfect. And I couldn't touch it without my head exploding.

"What about hair?" Shailene asked suddenly.

I blinked in confusion, jolted out of my thoughts about her skin. "What?"

She pulled her hair up as if she were putting it into a ponytail and held out a hank of it to me. "Maybe it won't hurt us if you try my hair. Providing this even works to begin with."

"Okay." I hesitated before slowly reaching out a hand. I wasn't sure which I was more worried about: the possibility that nothing would happen... or the possibility that something would.

I tentatively grasped the soft ends of her hair. When no pain stabbed between my eyes, I relaxed marginally. But my skin didn't change, either. What had I done earlier when my arm transformed? I'd been desperately trying to tap into my powers, find some way of getting away. *I just need to focus*, I told myself. *Concentrate on replicating the scenario from this morning.* I squeezed my eyes closed, willing something to happen.

My fingers tingled, warmth spreading up my arm. It burned—not painfully, but it wasn't exactly pleasant either. Then my muscles started to ripple, like I was rolling my joints involuntarily. Shailene gasped, and I opened my eyes just in time to see my face in the mirror change into someone else's.

Two Shailenes looked back at me in my reflection.

My breath came out sharply, and almost immediately my face started to morph back into itself. "No, no!" I cried, squeezing my eyes shut and focusing again. I felt my face shift again and then still. When I felt convinced that I was firmly in this form, I opened my eyes again.

"I can do it," I said, startled when the voice that came out was not my own. I even sounded like Shailene now. "I just have to make sure I don't get distracted. If I concentrate, I can hold it."

Shailene looked at me with a mixture of admiration and a tinge of fear in her eyes. "That's amazing," she said.

"Funny, I was going to say it was freaking weird," I replied.

"Well, yeah, that too."

I turned and looked at my reflection in the mirror from the side. Shailene was so much thinner than me, and a couple of inches taller. The difference in the way my body felt was disorienting. "Okay," I said. "We know I can do this now. So I think that's enough." I thought of my own body, and my flesh began to tingle once more, reforming back into my regular self. It was a relief to see my own face in the mirror again. Shailene may be hot, but I was happy being myself, thanks.

"So how do we use this to get to Janice?" Shailene asked.

"Yeah, about that." I gave myself one last look in the mirror, then turned to her, catching her dark eyes with my own. "I have an idea. It's risky, but I think we can pull it off."

She kept her gaze locked steadily on mine. "Whatever it is, I'm in."

I arched a brow. "Trust me that much?"

She smiled almost mischievously at me, and warmth spread through me, radiating out from my stomach.

"I do," she said.

"Excuse me? Hi."

The man looked up from his newspaper and quirked an eyebrow at me. He seemed so human sitting there on one of the station benches, reading a paper and waiting for his train. The part of me that had been just Ordinary Laura Clark three days ago was screaming at me that I was completely insane for thinking this guy was anything but a regular human.

But the New Laura Clark knew he wasn't. I focused on the squirming feeling in the pit of my stomach—my perception reminding me that something was different about this guy—and squared my shoulders.

"I need to talk to you," I said, flashing him my most disarming smile.

"I'm sorry?"

"You heard me." I hoped I sounded more confident than I felt. "I think you know who I am. And I definitely know who you are."

He looked from side to side, and for a panicked instant, I thought, *This is it. I was wrong. This isn't an Anesidoran. It's an ordinary human, and he's going to call a PeRT cop over, and I'm going to get arrested.*

Then he folded his newspaper closed and narrowed his eyes at me. "All right, Ms. Clark. What do you need to tell me?"

Holy shit. He really did know who I was. What was *up* with that?

Trying not to stammer, I said, "I, uh, I have some information about the last Striker. The one you guys are looking for."

He quirked his eyebrow again, and a slow smile spread across his lips. There was the slightest glimmer, and for an instant I could almost see the quiver of a mandible behind the façade, wiping away all of my remaining doubt. I tried not to gag.

"I'm listening," he said.

"Good," I replied. "But we can't talk here. Someone might overhear. The I.G.A. is watching me." I took a few steps and beckoned to him. "Come on."

The sentry followed me back toward the bathrooms. "This seems unnecessary," he said.

"Just humor me," I replied, looking around to make sure no one was watching. I still didn't understand the seeing/not seeing thing, and I didn't want to take any chances.

We stopped in front of a filthy set of trash cans, one for garbage and one for recycling, though it looked like people were throwing garbage in both cans without a care. People in PeRT stations are animals, I tell you.

"Okay. I came with you," the sentry said, tearing my attention away from the cans. "Now tell me. Where is the Striker?"

"Oh, the Striker?" I repeated, folding my arms. "She's right behind you."

Before he could react, Shailene clubbed him over the head with her electrified nightstick. The sentry screamed, his voice reverberating off the concrete floor and ceiling. I cringed and waited for a reaction, but no one came running. After several seconds' taut silence, I exhaled.

"All right," Shailene said, shooting me a grin that could only be described as rakish. "Let's get him tied up. Where are we going to hide him?"

"Back stall of the women's room," I said. "Hardly anyone uses this set of bathrooms. And even if someone comes in here, no one should be able to see him except one of us, right?"

Shailene nodded, and together, the two of us got the sentry tied up. He groaned a little as we started to drag him, but stayed unconscious.

"Okay," I said once we'd deposited him in front of the incredibly disgusting toilet. "Let's do this." I braced myself and, hesitantly, reached out to touch him. My skin burned with the now-familiar tingling sensation. I watched as my hand rippled into a claw, my arm into an armored shell. This felt weirder than when I'd turned into Shailene; it was more than just growing taller and fairer but otherwise staying human. This was changing my anatomy. I could feel my internal organs shifting, morphing into things they definitely shouldn't be.

Shailene watched me fretfully. "You okay?" she asked when the transformation was complete.

"Yeah," I said, my voice coming out in a deep, throaty growl. Shailene flinched. I turned, looking myself in the mirror, and immediately realized what Shailene meant when she said sentries don't *see* the way we do. Everything looked weird; it was all in black and white except for the red of Shailene's T-shirt. That was so vibrant it glowed. It was hard to make out the details of her face. She looked almost like a blurred silhouette. My own form, on the other hand, was clear to me, and it was pretty disgusting. But it was also flawless—there was no part of me remaining to give away that I was anything but this sentry. And that was the most important part of this plan. We needed to hide in plain sight. Shailene was the last Striker. They'd be coming for her. If we were going to turn the tides, we had to act now.

We had to find Janice and the others before the Anesidorans found Shailene. And what better way than letting them think they already had her?

"Remember the plan?" I said, trying not to wince at the sound of my own voice.

"Of course. We get on the train with the other sentries and go with them to wherever they're going. After all, I'm on Nibiru's side now, right?" She smiled, only looking ever-*so*-slightly like a Stepford Wife.

"Good. There should be another train coming along any time now, considering how many sentries there are prowling around out there." I watched as she pulled the stall door closed, shutting the unconscious sentry inside. "Let's just hope that the Anesidoran communication network is as disorganized as the I.G.A. seems to be. As long as they don't realize you're the one they're supposed to be looking for, we'll have a chance."

Shailene nodded. "It's a long shot, but it's the best we've got."

As we left the bathroom, I paused, looking around to make sure no one was watching us. Everything looked so bizarre through these alien eyes, and I felt weird just waltzing out into the station in this form. The Sentries usually disguised themselves when regular people were around. "You're sure no one can see me?" I asked.

"I'm sure," Shailene replied. "You're fine."

"Okay." I nodded. "Let's do this." We headed for the platform the ghost train had left from earlier. In our surveillance of the station after we'd come up with this plan, we'd noticed that there were at least a dozen sentries milling around the station. Another ghost train must be coming in soon—we'd just have to catch it.

As we started up the stairs, Shailene said in a quiet voice, "You know... you're pretty brave for an ordinary girl."

I stared at her. "Thanks, I guess?"

"I mean... Sorry, that came out wrong. What I meant is... It takes us Strikers years to get to the level where we're comfortable facing the Anesidorans head-on. Most people, when they find out what you have—it freaks them out for years. But you just took it in stride, and jumped right in to help us. I... I appreciate it, Laura. I'm sorry I was such a jerk when we first met."

Her words made me feel warm inside. I tried to grin, but found the mandibles my lips had shifted into didn't really work that way. I settled for a nod and a shrug.

When we reached the top of the stairs, another sentry was waiting for us. He was disguised as a human, a security guard like the first sentries I'd encountered on Thursday. But through my new eyes, I could see his true form superimposed over the top of the featureless human figure.

"Striker," he said, a note of suspicion in his voice. "What are you doing here?"

"Andronicus ordered me to meet up with the others," she replied coolly. "Is this the right floor?"

He glanced from her to me, then relaxed. My presence alongside her without any sign of distress, a sentry paired with a Striker just as Erikka had been earlier, seemed to ease his suspicion. "Yes, Platform C. Train should be coming in about five minutes."

She nodded, a self-assured arch to her eyebrow. Dismissing him. He moved away, reassuming his security guard façade of patrolling the deck. We moved over to Platform C, waiting for the train to pull in.

I looked around, still trying to get my bearings with these strange new eyes. A group of people was congregated across from us at Platform F, their features an indistinguishable blur to my eyes, as nondescript as bugs were (ordinarily) to me. Gray smears dotted here and there with unnaturally bright hues of neon red.

Under my breath, I murmured, "I was wondering... The sentries are able to disguise themselves as humans, like the security guards and that guy back there. So does that mean they're all bug things in disguise?" I kept thinking about Andronicus and the guy in the hood. The sentries were undisguised when they attacked us on the train, but those two—I'd only ever seen them in human form.

"No," Shailene replied, her voice barely audible. "Some of them are actually human." She paused. "Well, human-*ish*. There are different species on Nibiru. I didn't see them all when they... had me." I tried to focus on her face, but her expression was as blurry to me as if I were looking at her without my contacts on. "But of the ones I did see, some were humanoid, some weren't. Some were a hybrid." She shuddered. "But they were all monsters."

I turned, pacing a few steps away from her, trying to look casual. I almost didn't hear what she said next.

"The sentries were our precursors."

I turned back and stared at her, aghast. "You mean they used to be human?"

"No, no. They were grown in a lab. Cobbled together from a mix of Anesidoran DNA and creatures from Nibiru. Genetically-engineered monsters, with barely a brain to comprehend anything more than what they're programmed to do: serve the Anesidorans." She sighed, looking away. "That's what they want us to be. They honed every modification on them, but even with their ability to cloak themselves, it wasn't enough. They don't just want to rule humans. They want to change us."

"You mean, they want everyone on Earth to be like... us?" It still felt weird, lumping myself in with the Strikers. Even as I stood here in this insectoid body, clearly as far from being a normal human as it was possible to be.

"Yes. But no matter how much they experiment, removing our free will is too difficult. Or at least... it used to be."

The air began to vibrate with the sound of the approaching train. I could almost taste the sound in the air. Around us, other sentries in disguise stood up from benches where they'd been sitting, corners they'd been standing in. As they walked toward the platform, their disguises fell away, rippling off their bodies like a silky robe.

Moments later, the ghost train pulled into the station. I felt my skin tingle with anticipation as it slowed to a stop, and I closed my eyes, willing my heart rate to settle, forbidding myself to lose control of this transformation. After a couple deep breaths, the tingling sensation stilled. I opened my eyes and Shailene and I boarded the train.

I watched the other sentries for cues on how to behave. I supposed they weren't expecting me to guard Shailene, since as far as they were concerned, she was one of them. When Erikka had been standing alongside the sentries earlier today, I'd gotten the impression that they were less her guards and more her muscle. When they boarded the car, they spread themselves out, some sitting, others standing near windows, watching as the train swiftly began to pull out of the station. They didn't sit together, didn't make conversation amongst themselves. I thought about what Shailene had just said, about the sentries being grown in a lab. Did they really have so little personality that they didn't even talk off-the-clock?

I settled into an empty seat in the middle of the car. Shailene drifted toward the back, perching on a side-facing bench and looking out the window across from her. The train sped down the track in silence. I glanced at the stone-faced sentries around me. At least they were making this part of the plan easy on me. If they didn't want to talk, that made one less way for me to put my foot in my mouth and blow our cover.

I hadn't sensed Andronicus or the guy in the hood at all

since we'd lost Janice, but as the train pulled into the familiar valley where Erikka had confronted us, I felt a twinge behind my eye sockets. My breath caught in my throat. *No, dammit,* I thought.

But there was no mistaking it. Andronicus was close—getting closer every second. I turned casually, glancing out the window to my left, and saw a train approaching us on the opposing track. The ghost train. The same one Erikka and Janice had disappeared with earlier.

Maybe he's just heading back into the City, I thought, trying to steady my nerves. As long as that train passed us and kept on going, we'd be fine. He wouldn't catch us. By the time he figured out where we were, we might have already freed the other Strikers. It would be lucky, really.

Just pass us. Just pass us.

Suddenly my senses felt flooded. He was close—too close. The train jolted for a moment, and I realized with absolute certainty that he was here. He'd been on that other train, and he'd jumped to this one.

Andronicus was on our train.

I wanted to run over to Shailene, but I didn't dare make a scene. Slowly, my motions as controlled as I could make them, I stood, making my way down the aisle toward Shailene. She looked up at me, her expression blank but her eyes wide. I knew she couldn't sense him, but she must have guessed from that jolt and my reaction what I was trying to tell her.

We had to get away. We couldn't let him find her.

But before either of us could react, the door at the front of our car slid open and he stepped through, his trenchcoat whipping around him from the force of the air moving between the cars.

"That's her," he said in a loud voice, pointing at Shailene. "That's the one we're looking for. You idiots—"

Shailene caught my gaze for half a second. "Stay here. Don't get caught," she whispered. Before I could react, she'd broken away from me, racing to the back of the car and shoving the doors open. All around me, pandemonium erupted. There was an enormous *bang* as someone fired a weapon after her; it missed, ricocheting off the wall.

"Stop her!" Andronicus shouted, and without another moment's hesitation I raced after her. She'd told me to stay there, but there was no way I could.

She'd scrambled up onto the roof, two sentries hot on her heels. By the time I made it out there, she was fighting them off, brandishing her nightstick like a sword. I launched forward, intending to tackle the sentry closest to me, but then the sound of Andronicus' voice riveted me in place.

"Everybody freeze."

My feet obeyed against my will. I watched in horror as he pushed past me, striding casually toward Shailene.

"This ends now," he said. "Come here."

Shailene's eyes were wide, but she didn't fight him—she couldn't. Slowly, she closed the distance between them. I wanted to scream, cry, hurl myself at them like I had before, but this time I really couldn't move. His power was stronger than Erikka's had been. It was like a tractor beam. There was no escaping him.

He lifted his hand, fingers brushing against Shailene's face.

This can't be happening.

He pressed his thumbs to her temple.

No, I tried to scream, but the word wouldn't come. I couldn't even close my eyes. They were glued to the horror scene before me. He was going to erase Shailene, and this time there was nothing I could do. I braced myself for the flash of red lightning that would split the air in two.

But it didn't come.

"What is this?" Andronicus said, bewilderment clouding his features. He moved his hands across her face. Nothing happened. He stiffened, looking down at his hands, then back to Shailene. "This girl has already been altered. We'll have to take her back to the base to overwrite the existing protocol." He turned to me, and I felt his power on me loosen. "Sentry E-495," he said, in words I knew weren't English but I still understood. "Her inhibitor."

"I'm sorry?" I said. My brain thought the words in English, but they came out in something else entirely. What the *hell?* How was this happening?

Irritation spread across Andronicus' face. "I said, *her inhibitor.*"

I may have been able to speak his language, but I didn't know what any of that meant, or how to respond. Shailene still stood frozen in place, but her eyes locked with mine, panic flickering through them. *"Run,"* I could feel her silently urging me, but my feet wouldn't obey—not because of a spell this time, but because fear had rendered them completely useless.

"Sentry E-495—Wait a moment." His eyes narrowed. "You..."

"Run!" Shailene shouted out loud, and this time my feet obeyed me.

I turned, starting to dart across the roof of the train, but then Andronicus yelled, "Her inhibitor! Now!"

My brain barely registered the words when white-hot pain seared through my skull. I screamed, feeling my skin ripple with the shift back to my own body just as my knees gave out and I collapsed.

- Chapter 12 -

I couldn't move.

It wasn't that I was restrained (at least, I didn't think I was), but every part of me felt heavy. Like an invisible person was sitting on my chest and had tied lead weights to my wrists and ankles. Or like one of those dreams you have where you're half-awake and can see your room around you, but you can't move your body, can't get your lips to move in order to speak.

Finally I managed to open my eyes, staring up at a plain white ceiling and trying to figure out where I was and what I was doing there. There was a bad taste in my mouth, and my tongue felt fuzzy. How long had I been asleep?

As I lay there motionless, I could hear the muffled sound of someone talking, possibly in another room based on how quiet it was. I couldn't make out any words, though. Just the soft drone of a voice.

Eventually, enough feeling returned to my limbs that I was able to roll over onto my side. The crinkle of paper accompanied my movement, and I realized I was on an exam table. A doctor's office? I struggled to remember what I might have been doing that would have required a trip to the doctor, but my mind was a blur. I stared blankly at the wall across from me, which was covered with the sorts of posters you'd see in any physician's office. But as my eyes focused on them, I realized these weren't quite the pamphlets I was accustomed to. Instead of the typical fliers for cervical cancer screenings and BMI measurements, there were anatomy charts.

Non-human anatomy charts.

I stared in bewilderment at a cutaway of what looked like the musculature and organs of a minotaur. No joke. I blinked a couple times, trying to read what the text on the poster said before I realized it wasn't in English—or any alphabet I recognized, even. Next to it was another diagram that showed a blue-skinned cyclops with a horn protruding from its forehead.

When my eyes rolled confusedly to the next diagram, I suddenly realized with a jolt where I was—and why. The giant, insectoid figure was an Anesidoran sentry.

This wasn't a human doctor's office. It was an

Anesidoran one.

I sat up quickly, squeezing my eyes shut as a wave of dizziness washed over me. When it passed, I slid off the exam table and moved closer to the posters on the wall. The small room was covered with them, anatomy charts for half a dozen different alien species. Were these all Anesidorans?

I ran my fingers over the glossy paper. Some of these creatures were unfamiliar, creatures I'd never seen before; but many of them looked like monsters from Greek mythology.

Pandora's Box...

I shuddered and turned to the door. The last thing I remembered was the encounter on the train roof. If I was here, then where was Shailene? In another exam room? My stomach dropped through my feet as I remembered that she was the last of the cheerleaders who hadn't been captured. Had they brainwashed her yet? The way Erikka's personality had completely changed after the red lightning had struck flashed through my mind, and hysteria burbled up in my chest. They couldn't have erased Shailene. They just couldn't.

I had to find her. I had to save her. There must be a way to fix this.

Slowly, I approached the door, expecting to find a

sentry standing outside guarding to me. But to my shock, when I opened it the slightest crack, there was no one there. I was alone.

What the hell? This couldn't be right. There must be something holding me here. They wouldn't just leave me alone and unsupervised, right? I hesitantly raised my hand, expecting to hit an invisible forcefield when I started through the door, or some kind of electrical current—*something.* But to my shock, there was nothing.

I stepped out of the room into a narrow hallway, looking around myself in confusion. What was going on here?

The soft drone of someone talking was louder in the hall. I followed the sound of it, walking as quietly as I could, every nerve in me on edge. Any second now, someone would round the corner and bust me, I was certain of it. I looked anxiously over my shoulder before peering around a bend in the hallway.

There were two doors in the next corridor, both unguarded. The one directly ahead of me was closed, but to my right, the other door was slightly ajar. The voice I'd heard was coming from there. After a moment, I recognized it as Andronicus'. My blood ran cold.

"I'm just at my wit's end. This is completely unacceptable," he was saying to someone I couldn't see.

As softly as I could, I moved forward. If I was lucky, I might be able to creep past him to the door at the end of the hall, which I prayed was the exit.

"I've been making excuse after excuse to the council, but this is just too much. I don't know how I'm going to explain this to them. She acted in complete violation of the treaty. Your line agreed to stay out of the war, but she keeps interfering."

I was just tiptoeing past the door when the reply came. "I'm going to have to talk to her." It was a woman's voice.

A voice I recognized.

I froze in my place. It couldn't be. Goddammit, it just *couldn't*.

Shrinking back into the shadows, I peered around the door into the room. Andronicus had his back to me and was looking intently at some kind of webcam that was broadcasting onto a big TV screen.

And on the screen was my mother.

I miraculously managed to keep from making any noise, but I staggered back, my brain screaming an internal, monotone shriek of absolute horror.

It took a minute for my ears to catch back up, but eventually my mind processed that Andronicus was talking again. "You tried to talk to her the *last* time," he said, his voice dripping disdain. "Look where that got us. That's why we had to block her memories in the first place."

What?

I mean... *What?!*

"The implant was supposed to keep this from being an issue again. You assured us, Rose."

Mom gave him a look that she usually reserved for Tonio, or me, or any of our relatives when they got on her nerves. "Well, maybe it's malfunctioning, *Andre*," she snapped back. "Did you check it?"

Implant? They'd blocked my memories? I gripped the door frame until my knuckles turned white. My *mother* had blocked my memories?

"She was given a complete examination, and the implant was checked as well. It's in perfect working order."

Shailene. They'd erased Shailene from my memories. I really had known her before. I was convinced of it now. My *mom* was the one who'd erased Shailene. But why? And what else had they wiped from my mind?

"Well, maybe it needs an adjustment. Will it hurt her to have more memories blocked?"

Oh, my God. Oh, my *God*. It wasn't enough that they'd screwed around in my brain before, they were going to do it again.

"That doesn't resolve the issue at hand, though," Andronicus said. I barely heard him, my mind was reeling so hard. "The situation with Earth is extremely tense right now. The peace negotiations between our governments have gone from strained to... well, *nuclear* would work in both the metaphorical and literal sense. Our intelligence has discovered—"

I tried to pay attention to what he was saying, but I couldn't focus. If I just hung around here, they'd wipe my brain again. I'd forget about the Anesidorans. I'd forget everything that had happened this weekend.

I'd forget Shailene again.

No. Fuck that.

The more rational part of my mind told me I needed to get away from there as quickly as I could, escape before Andronicus got off Skype or whatever with my mom and noticed I was gone. But any rational thinking was being completely overridden by the fury growing in my chest. Rage at my parents and their secrets, at the Anesidorans for coming into my life and screwing it up not just once, but, apparently, multiple times. I didn't know who they were, or how they were related to me, or why they thought they could control me, but I was done playing their game. They weren't going to take me again, not without a fight.

I looked around for some kind of weapon. My eyes landed on a blue urn full of dried pussywillow branches on a table a few feet away from me. It seemed bizarrely normal, like the sort of thing you'd see in a regular human doctor's office, as opposed to some kind of secret alien health clinic, or whatever this place was. I grabbed the urn, pulling out the pussywillows and setting them silently on the table. Then I hovered in the doorway, watching.

Mom's face was gone off the screen. I hadn't heard her disconnect—in my anger, I'd stopped listening. Andronicus leaned back in his chair, closing his eyes and rubbing his temples. He seemed strained. How sad for him.

I didn't hesitate. In a swift, fluid movement, I shoved the door open, crossed the room in two steps, and slammed that urn down over his head as hard as I could. I was hoping it would break dramatically, but it just made a dull *thunk*. He let out a strangled cry and slumped in his seat.

I breathed out, setting the urn down and peering cautiously at his prone form. Blood was seeping from a cut on the top of his head, red like a human's. I didn't think I'd hit him hard enough to kill him, but I checked his pulse to make sure. He was alive, just unconscious. I needed to move quickly.

I swallowed and, squaring my shoulders, reached out and touched his face. My skin rippled, bubbling with warmth as it transformed. Even with the differences in anatomy, this change was not as severe as shifting into the sentry had been. Whatever Andronicus was, he really was closer to human than the other species of Anesidorans were.

Or, at least, closer to what *I* was. Whatever that may be.

As my skin changed, colors rippled across it, reminding me of my nightmare. In my dream, Andronicus had been standing over me, his face a kaleidoscope of colors. They danced across my flesh now, shifting and changing, before finally settling into the pale skin he usually wore. My heart pounded as I looked myself over. When I was satisfied the change was solid, I left Andronicus slumped in his chair, pulling the door closed behind me and striding down the hall as confidently as I could. If I encountered any other Anesidorans, I needed to be able to convince them that I was Andronicus. I needed to be calm, self-assured—smooth. I couldn't let my fear consume me, couldn't stop to dwell on my swirling thoughts, even though with every step I took, my mind screamed, "*Mom, Mom, Mom.*"

I'd known I had to be involved with this somehow—that my parents were involved. But not like this. Dad had worked for the I.G.A. He'd fought for Earth. He'd lost a partner. How could my mom have been talking to the Anesidorans like she was on their side? Like she was one of them?

"*The I.G.A. are not your friends.*"

No. This was wrong. It had to be wrong. There was some kind of misunderstanding, or this was some kind of mind game Andronicus was playing with me.

I couldn't think about it. Not now. I had to keep a cool head if I was supposed to find Shailene and get the two of us out of here. Of course, that was assuming she was still herself.

I refused to let myself believe otherwise.

The door at the end of the hallway opened onto a metal balcony inside what appeared to be a repurposed warehouse, or maybe an old airplane hangar. I glanced over the railing and reeled at the sight before me.

Spaceships. That's all they could be. They looked like sleek, black versions of the old space shuttles that sat in the Space and Military Museum in City West. Three of them sat side-by-side in the wide, open space below me. Suddenly I remembered what Andronicus had said before he'd realized who I was, when he hadn't been able to erase Shailene. *"We'll have to take her back to the base."*

Oh, my God. This wasn't just some random warehouse. This was the Anesidoran base.

Sentries milled about, moving boxes and crates down the gangplank of the ship on the far right. I tried not to gape at them. They were going about their business, and I needed to look like I was just going about mine. I glanced around quickly, trying to get my bearings. The balcony wrapped its way around the building, doors dotting the walls every few yards. Where would they be keeping Shailene? The medical wing had appeared to be deserted apart from me and Andronicus. He'd said that they needed to alter Shailene's implant, whatever that was. That sounded like a medical procedure. So if she wasn't where I'd just been, maybe they hadn't worked on her yet. If that was the case, she'd be in a holding cell or something, right? In a facility this size, there was sure to be some kind of brig.

I followed the balcony around the base's upper level, fighting the urge to hug the railing or shrink into the shadows. I was Andronicus. I owned this base.

A pair of sentries emerged from one door, saluting me as I passed. I nodded curtly at them, glancing beyond them as the door swung shut. A large, open space filled with boxes—some kind of storage area. Probably not what I was looking for. I kept moving.

On the opposite side of the hangar from the door I'd emerged through, a sentry armed with something that looked uncannily like a phaser stood in front of an otherwise nondescript door. Guarding it. That must be it. If they were still holding Shailene prisoner, she'd have to be guarded. Prisoners got guarded, right?

Unless they're prisoners named Laura Clark, apparently.

I swallowed.

"Sir," the sentry said as I approached, stepping aside to let me through. Andronicus must have been expected. I nodded at him as I had the other sentries and opened the door.

I wasn't sure what I'd expected on the other side of this door. A small room, maybe; some kind of closet that they'd have thrown Shailene into. But this—this was a *jail*. Cells lined the walls on both sides. They were all empty, their doors flung open wide, save the one in the back. A barred skylight dimly illuminated the room, casting stripes of light across her wan face.

I tried not to react at the sight of her. Beside me, the sentry said, "The test subjects have been loaded onto the transport ships already, sir. The Striker is the last one." He moved forward, unlocking the door to her cell. She crouched there, muscles tensed but otherwise unmoving.

"Good," I replied, hoping my voice held that same casual smoothness Andronicus always spoke with. "I'll handle her. Dismissed."

A beat of silence passed, my heart pounding in my chest while I chanted a thousand silent prayers that I'd said the right thing, that the sentry wasn't suspicious. Then he saluted, turning and closing the door behind him.

We were alone. I'd done it.

Shailene watched me warily as I stood in the open doorway of the cell, rising slowly to her feet. I stared at her, uncertain what to say, what to do. Had she been erased yet? Was I too late?

Finally, I managed to squeak out, "Are you still you?" The words sounded odd in Andronicus' voice.

She glared, the hatred in her eyes unmistakable. Nothing like the cool blankness of Erikka's eyes after the red lightning had struck. "Last time I checked."

Relief washed over me, and with it, something inside me unraveled. My skin began to ripple before I could stop it. I fought, for just an instant, to regain my grasp on the transformation, but it was like trying to hold on to water. It slipped between my fingers, and I was myself again.

"Laura," Shailene breathed, staring at me in disbelief.

I looked down at myself, then back up at her. "Hey," I said sheepishly. "Sorry it took me so long. Are you okay?"

She moved her lips wordlessly for a moment. Her eyes looked different than usual. Darker, shinier. I realized after an instant that it was because there were tears in them. Before I could react, she'd flung her arms around me.

Electric shock jolted through my body. I hissed, recoiling, as my vision went white.

IT WAS THE FIRST DAY of eighth grade, and it was way too hot to be allowed.

I managed to peel myself out of the crowd in the hallway and into the lab where my last-period science class was being held. I brushed my sticky hands off on my shorts. The first day of school, and already the air conditioner was broken. Everett was having a problem with vandals, our principal had informed us at the assembly this morning. Somehow they'd managed to climb up onto the roof and steal the copper out of the air conditioning unit. A pretty penny for them, and no cool air for us. It seemed to me that the reasonable solution would have been to cancel school—after all, it was supposed to reach a hundred and nine today, and the last thing they wanted was for their precious students to get heat exhaustion, right?—but of course not. School was too important. We just had to roast.

"Sit anywhere you like," the teacher said from in front of the whiteboard. "I'll be announcing your lab partners and assigned stations after the bell."

Sigh. Assigned partners. Of course. I glanced around the room. My friend Charlotte waved at me from the back. It was too bad we wouldn't be able to pick our own partners. Charlie was a total science geek, and it definitely wasn't my top subject.

I dropped my backpack onto the floor and clambered up onto the tall stool beside her. I pulled my glasses off, setting them to one side, slumping forward and resting my cheek on the cool granite countertop. "How are your classes?" I asked. I barely had enough energy to move my mouth and speak.

"Fine," she said, fanning herself with her composition notebook. "I'm just ready for this day to be over."

"Me too," I said, turning my face to rest the other cheek on the granite. The stool next to me was empty, but a girl I didn't recognize was sitting in the one beside that, in the back corner of the room. She had black hair that curled around her shoulders, and skin as pale as a sheet of paper. She looked like Snow White or something.

My stomach flip-flopped, and I turned my face back the other way, hoping she hadn't seen me looking. I had only recently figured out that I was more interested in staring at girls than at boys, and she wasn't the first girl I'd seen that had made my cheeks burn.

But she was definitely the prettiest.

The bell rang, and I sat up, eyeing the teacher warily.

"Good afternoon, everyone. I hope you're all surviving this somewhat hellish weather. Though I should tell you now"—he gestured at the various kids around the room who were fanning themselves with folders, compositions books, and even their open hands—"doing that actually doesn't cool you off. The energy you expend with the fanning motion just generates more heat and raises your body temperature. So if you could place your papers back on your worktops, we can get started. To begin, your lab partners..."

He looked down at the planner on his desk and started rattling names off. He called everyone by their last names, like it was boot camp or something. I watched as my classmates moved around the room around me. Charlotte got paired with a kid with glasses who was about half her height. I should have known it would be too much to hope that we'd have gotten paired together. I just hoped my new partner wouldn't be a jerk.

"Clark-without-an-E?"

I jolted in my seat. "Laura?"

"Yes. You're with Maximoff."

I looked around, uncertain who that was. I'd known everyone at my elementary school, but Everett Middle was a lot bigger. Apart from the kids I'd had classes with last year, I didn't know that many people.

Two seats away from me, the Snow White-looking girl caught my eye. Her face was gaunt and wary-looking. "Hey," she said, shoving her backpack across the floor with her foot and getting up to take Charlotte's empty seat.

Oh. So this was Maximoff.

I avoided her gaze as she sat down beside me, hoping the heat was helping disguise my blush. My face had definitely been red enough from it all day.

The two of us sat silently for a minute while the teacher called out the rest of the names. When it became obvious she wasn't going to be the first one to talk, I took the leap. "Did you know you have the same last name as the Scarlet Witch?" I said. "She's my favorite X-Man. Er, X-Woman. X-Person."

I wasn't sure how she would react to this, but to my relief, she grinned crookedly. Warmth spread from my fingers to my toes. "Really?" she said. "That's cool, I guess. I hate my last name."

I didn't know how to react to that. I'd never really thought about my last name, or whether it was likable or not. It just was. "Well, what about your first name?"

She made a face, like something smelled bad. "I hate my first name even more than my last name."

I frowned. What kind of person was this that the teacher had partnered me with? "What is your first name?"

"Ivanka."

I grimaced. "Yikes. Can't say I blame you." She looked down, and I jumped to change the subject. "Well, what should I call you? Do you have a different name you like?"

The girl shrugged. "I have a name I like, but it's dumb. It's not my real name."

"Of course it's not dumb!" I said. "People should call you what you want to be called."

She looked up at me with a surprised expression. "Really? You don't think it's weird?"

I grinned, showing off a mouthful of braces. "Definitely not. So what should I call you?"

Her face looked red. It was ninety degrees inside, after all, I told myself.

"Shailene," she said. There was weight to the word when she said *it, like speaking it out loud made it official. Like she'd declared, This is who I really am, and the words had bent the universe, forcing it to accept it.*

I nodded, smiling. "Shailene is a pretty name. It suits you."

SHE PULLED AWAY FROM ME, eyes wide. Both of us were struggling for air. She braced herself against the bars of the cell, her shoulders moving up and down with her labored breathing.

"I'm sorry," she said, pushing the heel of her hand against her eye. "I forgot. I was just so relieved to see you…"

"It's okay," I said, squeezing my own eyes closed, inhaling through my nostrils. That had been a memory. That was one of the memories that I'd been missing. That my *mom* had taken from me.

Had Shailene seen the same thing?

Now wasn't the time to ask her. We had to get out of here. I couldn't dwell on it, couldn't think about what I'd just seen… couldn't wonder about what else was hiding in my mind.

I looked down at my hands in frustration. "How are we

supposed to escape if I lost Andronicus' form? I'd been hoping we could just walk out..."

Shailene brushed off the knees of her filthy workout pants and clenched her fist. "The old-fashioned way. Speed and brute force."

I grimaced. "Awesome. My favorite."

She nudged my side with her elbow, careful not to make any skin contact. "You'll be fine. But we'll have to move fast, before they get a chance to figure out what's going on." She moved to the door, opening it the tiniest crack and then silently closing it. "That sentry is still out there," she whispered.

"What? I told him 'dismissed'!" I protested.

"Well, apparently that just meant 'leave the room' to him. It's fine, I've got this." Before I could blink, she'd ripped the door open, grabbed him in a stranglehold, and pulled him back into the room. The door swung shut behind them.

I jumped forward, grabbing it just before it slammed. "Are you freaking serious?" I snapped.

Shailene had her legs wrapped around the sentry's torso, holding his mandibles closed with her hands, keeping him from making any noise apart from a muffled grunt. The creature fought to buck her off him, and his gun went skittering across the floor.

"Grab that!" Shailene ordered, and I darted to obey. I jumped upright, aiming the weapon at the sentry, unsure if I was holding it correctly, or even where the trigger was. "Are you trying to kill me?" she shrieked. "Give me that thing!" In a fluid motion, she snatched the gun out of my hands and kicked the sentry away from herself. He staggered backward and she brandished the weapon. There was a flash of light, and he collapsed.

I blinked at her. "Since when can you do that?"

"Since always?" She tossed her head, her hair flying out of her face. "I'm an I.G.A. Striker. Or did you forget that?"

"Well, why didn't you do it earlier?"

She gawked at me. "When, in the train station? With two dozen other sentries around us, hiding in plain sight? I'm a Striker, not a one-woman army."

I rolled my eyes and poked the sentry with my foot. "Is he dead?"

"I don't think so. It was set to stun." She looked the weapon over. "I think."

"Okay. Let's get the hell out of here before he or Andronicus wakes up, then." I shoved his crumpled form into one of the empty cells, then crouched, placing my hand on him and shifting quickly. It felt less strange the more often I did it.

Shailene watched me. "I wish I could do that," she said as I closed the cell door. "It would make getting out of here a whole lot easier."

I wanted to smile at her, but once again my mutated facial muscles wouldn't cooperate. I wondered how sentries were able to disguise themselves as humans so easily. Was it something like my own power? That thought made me queasy, so I pushed it aside. "Don't worry. I'll protect you."

She cocked an eyebrow. "*You'll* protect *me?*"

"Fine. We'll protect each other."

That made her smile. She brandished the gun and nodded. "All right. We'll protect each other."

I opened the door, looking around to make sure it was clear. "Okay, let's go. Where are we going?"

"This facility is built into the side of the mountain. That hangar door"—she gestured—"opens out to the air. But there are a few ground-level exits up here. They brought us in through one of them. You were... not awake." She shuddered and shook her head. "Um, anyway, there's a large storage room, and there's a driveway to let trucks in and out."

"I know where that is. Come on."

We hurried across the balcony. This level was mostly

deserted, but I tried to block Shailene's form from the hangar level as best I could with my body. Nerves racked me, but beside me, gripping that gun, Shailene looked confident, unflappable.

I opened the door to the storage room I'd seen before, the one the two sentries had emerged from. It looked empty. I waved Shailene in. "Stay behind those boxes," I said, gesturing to a stack of crates along the wall. "I'll make sure that our exit route is clear."

The room was a maze of storage containers. Huge crates, big enough to hold a person, towered up to the ceiling. I wound my way between boxes, peering around cautiously. I could hear voices somewhere in the room. If we were going to get out of here undetected, we'd have to get rid of them first.

I rounded a corner to see three sentries unloading crates from the back of a truck. One of them looked up. "L-193, what are you doing here?" he asked in their bizarre language.

"Andronicus took charge of the Striker," I replied.

"Good. You can help us unload these. We need them brought down to C-level."

I hesitated, unsure what to do. We didn't have time to waste on me moving boxes for the Anesidorans. But if I protested now, the others would be suspicious. The sentry stared at me expectantly, and I moved forward to take a box off the back of the truck.

Before I had a chance to worry about where, exactly, C-level was, I heard a door bang open back where we'd come from. My heart leapt into my throat. Where was Shailene? They hadn't caught her, had they?

Footsteps approached rapidly, and then he came around the corner. The guy in the hood from earlier—but his hood was off now.

It took all the strength I had not to lose my transformation. I could feel my skin crawling, threatening to ripple back to human flesh, and I closed my eyes, screaming at every cell in my body to stay right where it was.

"All of you, come with me," he barked. "We need all the sentries from this quadrant in the medical wing. Laura Clark has gone missing. She hasn't had her implant modified yet. We have to find her before she leaves the facility."

"Yes, sir," the other sentries around me said, and I joined them in the salute I'd seen them use earlier. The other three hurried after him, and I followed. But when they turned a corner in the labyrinth of boxes, I pulled back, my heart pounding as I shrank into the shadows of a stack of crates. My tenuous hold on the transformation slipped, and I curled into myself, trying to calm the panic racing through my veins, the utter rejection of seeing yet another freaking person I knew in this goddamned facility.

Tall, muscular, olive-skinned. Impeccably handsome with sleek, gelled hair. Just as much a movie star as Andronicus and his Cary Grant-style debonair. I'd sensed him the morning Erikka had been captured, and again when he'd confronted us on the train, and I still hadn't been able to connect the dots. But now it seemed so obvious I wanted to kick myself.

Damien. Damien was an alien.

Someone tapped my shoulder, and I almost screamed. I jerked my head back and saw Shailene standing over me, the gun still clenched in her hand.

"Oh, thank God," I whispered back when I'd caught my breath. "They didn't find you."

"Are you okay?" she asked, peering at my bloodless face.

"That guy. I know him." I struggled back up to my feet. "That's my big's boyfriend."

"Your 'big'?"

"Big sister. In my sorority. See, when you join a sorority, they assign you an upperclassman to show you the ropes and stuff. They call it *bigs* and *littles*." I shook my head. "Never mind. It's not important. We need to get out of here, and I have to warn Ana."

The storage room was deserted. We hurried back over to the truck the sentries had been unloading and Shailene scrambled up into the cab. We needed to get out of here before somebody figured out what was going on and caught up with us. I couldn't let this rattle me. If I could handle the fact that my own freaking *mother* was involved with an alien invasion, I could deal with Ana's douchebag boyfriend.

"The key's in the ignition," Shailene called down to me.

"We need to get this open," I called back, looking up at the heavy metal door in front of us. There was a control panel with a touch screen attached to it.

"If that's anything like the ones in their other facilities, it only responds to Anesidoran DNA," Shailene said, following my gaze. "If a human tries to activate it, an alarm will go off." She brandished the gun. "Should I shoot it out?"

"Will that keep the alarm from going off?" I asked.

"Probably not."

I cursed under my breath. Then I looked down at my hand, and thought about how I'd been able to respond when the sentries had talked to me in that weird, other language. The fact that I could shapeshift when none of the other human experiments could.

But the sentries could.

For some reason, I'd felt weirder about seeing Damien here than seeing my mom. I figured that was because I'd already begun to guess my family was wrapped up in this. But what if it was more than that?

Maybe it was those repressed memories lurking beneath my skin. Maybe they weren't buried as deep as I'd thought—maybe they lurked just beneath the surface of my subconscious.

Maybe I'd known this all along.

I pressed my hand against the panel. Shailene made a noise of protest behind me, but no alarm came. The door shuddered, then started to rumble open.

There it was. The answer. The one that had been staring me in the face this whole time. That I'd tried to deny, to block from my mind.

I was involved. Because I was *one of them*. My mom was talking to Andronicus... because *she* was one of them.

I was Anesidoran.

"Laura," Shailene said, still leaning out of the cab of the truck. I couldn't look at her.

"Let's just get out of here," I said.

- Chapter 13 -

We drove the truck halfway down the hillside before abandoning it. We couldn't take the risk of the Anesidorans being able to track the vehicle. When we left the base, the sun was shining brightly overhead—a night and half a day had passed while I'd been unconscious in that doctor's office, while Shailene rotted in that prison cell. By the time we made it out of the hills and into a small farmtown nestled along a country highway, the sun was already starting to set.

We followed the main street until we found a small café. The sign said they were open until eight o'clock. When we stepped inside, a clock on the wall showed we had forty-five minutes left until then.

"Excuse me," Shailene said, approaching one of the baristas standing behind the counter wiping off mugs with a dishrag. "Our car broke down…"

I shuffled over to a table, sinking into the worn wooden chair. Every bone in my body ached. I wanted to go home and take a nice, hot bubble bath. Then I wanted to go to sleep in my own bed—*my* bed, in my house, not the hard dorm-style bed at the Gam-Lam house—and wake up in the morning and have my mom there, and my dad, and Lola and Tonio, and have everything be back to normal. No aliens. No missing memories. No lies. I squeezed my eyes shut, trying not to cry.

"Can I get you something, hon?" The other barista had come over to the table, a notepad in her hand.

I shook my head, shoving a strand of hair behind my ear. "I lost my wallet."

She looked at me sympathetically. "You two have had a day. It's on the house."

"Really?" I smiled tightly. "Thank you. Can I have a cinnamon latte?"

She patted my shoulder and left to make my drink. I watched as Shailene talked to the barista behind the counter. At one point, he handed her his cell phone. I slumped forward, resting my face on the cool table until the woman came back with my latte.

It was almost gone by the time Shailene made it over to the table. "He let me use his phone to log in to Lyft. I got us a ride back to your sorority house. They should be here before the café closes. We'll check on your big, and then we can figure out to do from there."

I nodded but didn't say anything.

Shailene sat down across from me. "Laura," she said.

"Please don't." I couldn't look at her. I clutched the ceramic mug tightly between my hands, swishing the remnants of my coffee around and feeling sick to my stomach.

"No. I have to." She reached over, folding her fingers over the top of the cup, just centimeters from mine. It sent jolts through me, as if she'd laid her hand over mine. "Laura, whoever you are... it's okay."

"It's okay?" I looked up at her, my eyes stinging. I swallowed the tears back, burning my throat. "I'm Anesidoran, Shailene. And that's okay?"

"Yes." Her gaze didn't waver from mine. "Everything we've gone through has proved that. I don't know what's going on with you or your family, but it's not important. I trust you."

I blinked, and a hot tear coursed down my face. It couldn't be okay, just like that. But she said it was, and she meant it. More than anything in the world, I wanted to take her hand in mine. But I couldn't even do that, thanks to my mom. I squeezed the mug even tighter instead.

My family had caused this. What had happened to Shailene and hundreds of other people around the world. And now even Ana was in danger, and it was all my fault. She had asked me to go to dinner with them last night, and I hadn't even answered her. I could have been there as a buffer, tried to protect her from Damien somehow. But instead I'd ignored her. And now I didn't even have my phone to check and see if she was all right.

Our Lyft driver pulled up just as the café was closing for the evening. He was chatty and chipper, but I wasn't in the mood for talking. Shailene gave him the same story that she'd given the baristas—that our car had broken down outside of town, and we needed a ride back to campus while it was in the shop.

"That's the worst. You guys look like you've had a hell of a day," the driver said sympathetically. He was the second one to say something to that effect. I was scared to look at myself in the mirror now. When I didn't respond, he carried on enthusiastically, "So, you go to St. Francis, too?"

"She does. I go to Bayview," said Shailene.

"Ooooh," the driver roared. "I don't know if I can ferry a Swordsman in my car. Nah, just kidding. You're okay. But you better watch out, with two Mariners here with you. I was just heading back over to campus. Sucks that spring break is over already. Did you guys do anything fun?"

He carried on like that until we made it back to City East. By the time we pulled up in front of the Gam-Lam house, my stomach was tied up in tight, nervous knots. I raced up the walkway, hurriedly typed in my passcode to the front lock, and flung the door open.

Immediately I was greeted by pandemonium. I realized belatedly that if we'd spent the night in the Anesidoran base, today was Sunday—everyone was back from spring break now. Classes started again tomorrow. The front entryway echoed with laughter and squealing voices.

"Wow," Shailene said, taken aback. "How many girls are in this sorority?"

"A hundred and twenty. The house sleeps about ninety of us. The seniors usually like to get apartments off-campus, and the rest are studying abroad this semester."

Shailene didn't say anything. Her mouth was frozen in an *O*-shape. I looked around the entrance to my house, trying to remember how I'd felt the first time I'd come through these doors. It had only been eight months ago, but it felt like a lifetime. I supposed it could seem imposing if you weren't used to it. The house had been built right after the Great Fire had wiped out half the city, and the dark, heavy wood beams that held up the ceiling had been salvaged from a mansion that had burned down. To the right, our formal living room where alumnae held their association meetings was currently overflowing with girls back from vacation, who hadn't even bothered to take their suitcases upstairs before congregating together to gossip and share what had gone on over the week and a half they'd been away. The doors to the date room were open in front of us, though the room was empty—back in the day, girls would bring their dates to that room, and the high threshold of the doors would let the house mom check to make sure that everyone's feet were still on the floor and no hanky panky was going on. Nowadays, we used the room as a library, and a display case between the shelves held the awards our chapter had received over the years.

To the left was a hallway leading to the main staircase, the kitchen and dining area, and the house mom's room. I gestured to Shailene to follow me that way now. We'd made it up all of three steps when I heard Claudia, our house mom, call my name.

"Laura, there you are."

"Oh, hey, Claudia," I said, turning to face her. Plump, cheery-faced and in her mid-thirties, she was less of a *mom* and more of... well, not quite a sister. Maybe a relatively chill aunt? "Did you have a nice vacation?"

"I did. Who's that with you?"

Shailene, who'd frozen on the steps beside me, put on her polite face. "Hey, nice to meet you," she said, coming back down the stairs to shake Claudia's hand. "I'm Shailene. I'm a friend of Laura's."

"A friend?" Claudia repeated, a loaded tone in her voice, and I felt my face turn three different shades of red. She couldn't be serious here.

Oh, but she was.

"Laura, dear," she said, "is she just a *friend* friend? Or is she a... *special* friend? Because, you know, rules are rules. No paramours upstairs, regardless of gender—"

"Jesus, Mary, and Joseph!" I shrieked, wanting the stairs to open up like a crocodile jaw and just swallow me down. "She's just a friend!"

"Okay, okay," Claudia replied, holding her hands up. "I'm just doing my job."

"Fine, whatever. Have you seen my big?" I couldn't bring myself to look in Shailene's direction.

"No, I haven't. But it's been helter skelter around here. Try her room?"

I bolted up the stairs without another word, Shailene following behind. "That was interesting," she said, the hint of a laugh in her voice.

"If by 'interesting' you mean 'the most mortifying

experience of my life', then sure."

"Oh, come on, Laura," she said. "You have to admit it was a little funny."

Funny that she thought we'd be a couple? I wondered. Or just funny in a cosmic sort of way? Shailene's face didn't give away anything, but her ears looked the slightest bit pink.

Probably a sunburn, I told myself, and hurried down the hallway.

"Which room is yours?" Shailene asked as we squeezed past a group of sophomores whose names I didn't know. One thing about having a hundred-plus girls in a club, there was no way you could get to know everyone.

"Oh, I'm in one of the porches," I answered.

She blinked. "You sleep on a *porch*?"

"Well, it's not actually a porch." I laughed. "They just call them sleeping porches. I'm not sure why. It's more like... Here, I'll show you." I detoured away from the staircase I'd been heading toward and gestured her into my room.

"Laura!" Gail, one of my roommates, squealed, jumping up from her bed and running over to give me a hug. She, Marisleysis, and Sierra were the only ones in the room, the three of them piled up on Mari's bed watching a movie on her laptop. But I could see from the mess of open suitcases and clothes strewn over everyone else's beds that all my roommates were back.

"Wow," Shailene said behind me. "This looks like the bedroom of the twelve dancing princesses." She gestured to the two rows of beds. "Where's the secret passage you use to get to the magical kingdom every night?"

"Hilarious," I sniped. "Gail, have you seen my big?"

"I haven't seen her, but she left a note on your whiteboard," she said, giving Shailene a curious look before scampering back over to the bed.

"Thanks." I maneuvered around the island of desks in the middle of the room to my own. My whiteboard was propped against the hutch where I'd stacked a few books and my mountain of CDs. In blue marker, Ana had written:

Little—

My texts aren't going through anymore. I figure you forgot to charge your phone again. I hope you aren't mad at me. Please understand, I wasn't trying to keep secrets from you. When you get back, coffee?

Ana.

I stared at her flowery handwriting with its large, rounded loops, and tried to choke back the emotion burbling up in my throat.

Beside me, Shailene picked up a stack of CDs, flipping through them. "This is pretty old-school," she commented.

I shrugged. "I have pack rat tendencies."

"I see that. And you like boy bands. New Kids On The Block, Backstreet Boys..." She turned one over and snickered. "Seriously? One Direction?"

I snatched it out of her hands before I could stop myself, my heart suddenly feeling like it was clawing its way out my chest. Ana had given me that One Direction CD in one of her secret care packages last semester—before I'd known just who my mysterious sister really was, when she'd heard how much I liked boy bands. After initiation, we'd karaoked shred versions of all the songs on the album while our sisters had laughed raucously around us.

"*I wasn't trying to keep secrets from you,*" she'd written. But I had. I'd been keeping secrets from her for days. She was my best friend, my *sister*, and I'd pushed her away when I needed her the most. How could I have left her alone like this?

"Let's go check in her room," I said raggedly.

I led Shailene up the stairs to the third floor, where Ana's room was. She had a double, but the junior she'd roomed with last semester was studying abroad this semester, so the other bed was empty. I knocked on the door, but there was no answer. Hesitantly I pushed it open.

The room was empty, Ana's bed neatly made like it had been the other day. She wasn't there.

"Don't panic," Shailene said, watching my expression. "She might be here. Does she have any other friends in the house? She might be with them."

"Yeah, the Deltas," I said, rushing down the hall to where Natalia and Makeisha's room was. I could hear voices and laughter drifting from their open door, and for a moment, relief washed over me. But then I stuck my head in the doorway and saw that it was just those two and their own littles back from break.

"*There* you are, chickie," Natalia all but shouted. "Where the hell have you been? You look like you've been hit by a semi."

"It's a long story." I sighed. "Don't give me that look. I'm fine. Where's my big?"

Makeisha raised her eyebrows and shared a glance with Natalia. "There's the question. You've been missing the hanky-panky, girl."

I felt the blood leave my face. "What?"

"She went off with that Beta of hers. Said there was some kind of family emergency. Their dog needed to have surgery or some other bullshit lie that we all saw through. She said she might be gone for a few days, she and the BF were going to 'pet-sit'"—she made air quotes—"the other animals for his parents."

"*What?*"

Natalia glared at Makeisha. "Come on, you don't *know* it was a bullshit lie. After all, you know how Ana is about animals. I wouldn't put it past her to cut school for a few days to pet-sit."

"Yeah, but why would his parents be gone for a few days if a *dog* is having surgery? They're not going to let them sleep at the vet, and I don't think the Ronald McDonald House puts up pet owners."

Makeisha's little spoke up. "You never know. My dog had hip dysplasia, and we had to take her down south for her evaluation—"

I couldn't take any more of this. "Let me use your phone," I interrupted, my voice shrill.

"Where's yours?" asked Makeisha.

"I lost it."

"Again?" Natalia shook her head. "Am I going to have to get you one of those key beepers for your birthday? One for your wallet, one for your phone..."

"Just let me use your phone!" I shrieked.

Makeisha tossed me hers without another word, and I raced back out into the hall, scrolling through Makeisha's contacts and frantically dialing Ana's number. It rang once, then went to voicemail. Dammit. I quickly typed out a text.

Ana, this is Laura. I don't have my phone. Please call ASAP.

I hit send and waited. A few moments later, a red exclamation point flashed on the screen. *Message Delivery Failure.* I let out a growl of frustration. He had her. Damien had her. What was I going to do?

"Hey," Shailene said, her voice soft. I jumped; I'd forgotten she was standing next to me. She looked at me, her eyebrows drawn with worry. "You okay?"

"I don't know," I said, my voice breaking. "I don't know what to do."

She folded her arms slowly, looking down at her feet. "I know exactly how you feel," she whispered. And I knew she did. This is just what she'd been going through, losing the other cheerleaders, losing Janice. I couldn't have possibly understood. Not until it had happened to me.

"She's really important to you, huh?" Shailene asked.

I nodded, sniffling. "She's like... It's like Janice, I guess. I mean, I know it's not, because Janice is your mom, but Ana's like..." I stared up at the fluorescent lights on the ceiling. "You know when you find someone you didn't realize you were looking for until they're there? And they become your family, and you realize... without them there's a big hole." I swallowed. "And I've been ruining it. I've been so pissy and moody ever since all of this started." Since I'd met Shailene. But no, Shailene was only part of it. It was Damien. I'd been jealous of him. Not romantically, but jealous that he was spending time with her. Afraid he'd take her away from me. Even though Ana had tried to include me, I hadn't wanted any part of it. And now she was gone, and it was all my fault. If I'd gone to breakfast with her, if I'd met them for dinner—I would have sensed what he was, I knew it. I could have warned her, could have protected her. Instead I'd been selfish, and it could cost her her humanity.

"It's not your fault, Laura," Shailene said.

"Yes, it is." It was. In more ways than one. It wasn't just that I'd left her alone, it was that my family—*I*—was somehow involved in this. My mom was possibly complicit with these kidnappings, these experiments. Whatever was going to happen to Ana, it was all my fault. In every way.

I had to stop this. There still had to be time. I could save her.

And I had an idea as to how.

"We'll find a way to get her back, Laura," Shailene said, cutting through my thoughts. "We'll think of something."

"Yeah, you're right," I said. I didn't mention that I'd already thought of something. But it was way too dangerous to bring Shailene along. I couldn't let her get near the Anesidorans again, not when they were planning to erase her.

I smiled casually. "We'll think about it in the morning. It's been a long two days, and both of us are beat. I don't know about you, but I need a nice, long shower."

"You're not the only one," Shailene said.

My face flushed, and I tried to keep my thoughts from wandering in the direction that sentence took me. "Where are you going to stay tonight? It's probably not safe to go back to Bayview, or wherever you and Janice live."

She bit her lip. "Probably not."

"We have a guest room downstairs by Claudia's apartment. We can make up some excuse as to why you can't make it back to campus tonight. I'm sure she'll let you stay."

Shailene nodded. "That's a good idea."

"Come on," I said. "Let's get you set up." I led her back into Natalia and Makeisha's room, briefly introducing her and explaining that she was a friend who had gotten stranded due to a broken-down car. "I'm going to ask Claudia if she can stay in the guest room. Natalia, any chance she could borrow some of your clothes?" They were about the same height and looked like they'd wear the same size.

"Sure thing," Natalia said. "I'll get you set up."

She led Shailene down the hall to the wardrobe room, where all the girls who lived in the small, closet-less doubles kept their clothes. While they rummaged through Natalia's drawers, I quickly typed out another text, to a number I knew by heart.

This is Laura. Don't respond to this because I don't have my phone. Just get your ass to the Gam-Lam house by 11 if you ever want me to speak to you again. I thought for a moment, then added, *And not one word to my mom.* As soon as the delivery checkmark appeared, I deleted both messages off Makeisha's phone and handed it back to her.

I showed Shailene to the second-floor bathroom. "The plumbing is old, so if someone comes in here, they'll yell that they're flushing and you can step out of the water before you get scalded," I said, pulling aside the shower curtain on one of the stalls and looking it over to make sure it wasn't completely disgusting.

Shailene looked like she was having trouble keeping her mirth to herself. "This is a very interesting living situation," she said dryly.

I let out a snort. "Tell me about it. Here." I handed her a comb. "You can use this to comb your hair out when you're done. I promise I don't have lice." I set it on top of the neatly folded clothes she'd placed on the bench inside the shower, in the little changing area where the water didn't hit.

"Gee, thanks," she said sarcastically, then caught my eye. "But seriously. Thanks."

My cheeks colored. "You too," I said.

BY THE TIME Shailene got out of the shower, I'd gotten clearance from Claudia that she could stay, and the guest room was unlocked. I showed her inside. "If you think you'll be okay by yourself for a little bit, I'm going to take a shower now." She'd tossed her dirty clothes on the bed in a heap, and I picked them up gingerly. "I need to do a load of laundry later, so I can wash these up for you if you want."

"Yeah. Thanks, Laura," she replied with a smile.

I smiled back at her. "See you in a bit."

I closed the guest room door and hurried back up the stairs to the bathroom. She'd set my comb on the bathroom counter. She'd cleaned it out, but there were still a couple strands of hair wrapped around the plastic teeth. I just prayed they weren't my own. I grabbed it, ducking into the empty shower stall. I stripped out of my own clothes and quickly pulled her grimy workout clothes from yesterday on. The pants were way too tight on my hips, but the stretchy fabric had enough give to it that I managed to get them up over my butt. I clutched the comb, closed my eyes, and concentrated.

My body shifted effortlessly.

When I stepped out of the shower, I refused to let myself be startled by her reflection in the mirror. I gave myself just a cursory once-over to make sure that the change had taken completely, that no part of Laura remained. Then I rushed out of the bathroom.

Back at the Anesidoran base, the cells had all been empty. The sentry had said to me, *"The test subjects have been loaded onto the transport ships already."* If Damien had abducted Ana for the Anesidorans to experiment on—and I was certain that he had—she would be with them. If I wanted to free her, I had to find a way to get aboard one of those ships.

I had to go back to the base.

- Chapter 14 -

I was already standing on the sidewalk when Tonio's steel gray Oldsmobile turned into the street. I waved frantically as he approached, flinging the door open before the car had come to a complete stop.

"Thank God, you got my text," I said, slamming the door shut and buckling my seatbelt. Then I turned to see him staring at me with an expression of bewilderment. "What?"

"Uh, who the hell are you?" he said.

Crap. I'd forgotten already that I was in Shailene's form. I couldn't morph back, either, because then I wouldn't be able to get her back—I'd left the comb in the bathroom like an idiot. "Tonio," I began, "I know this is probably really, really weird, but I can explain..."

He rolled his eyes and shook his head. "Laura. I should

have known. So you're doing that again, huh?"

"*'That'?* Oh, you mean—Have I done it before?"

He pulled away from the curb, driving down the hill away from campus. "I'm not getting involved. Where do you want me to take you?"

"Head for the interstate. I'll give you directions as we go. And you sure as hell are getting involved. You're already involved, obviously. How much do you know, anyway?"

He looked at me sideways, pursing his lips. "How much do *you* know?"

I ground my teeth in exasperation. "Seriously, Tonio?"

"Yes, seriously." He flipped on his turn signal, barely looking over his shoulder before charging into the left lane. The first rule of driving in the City was that it wasn't for the meek. "I'm going to be in deep enough shit with your mom when I get home—not to mention *mine*. I'm not supposed to talk about this with you."

"Fine. *I'll* tell *you*, then." I gave him an account of everything that had happened over the last four days, culminating in our escape from the Anesidoran base and discovering that my DNA could open the lock.

"So that means... I'm part Anesidoran," I finished in a small voice.

"Well, yeah," Tonio replied. He seemed unperturbed.

I stared at him incredulously. "What do you mean, 'well, yeah?' So you knew about all this? You knew that I'm... that I'm part alien?" Saying the words aloud was harder than I would have expected. Even with all the crazy things happening to me, it was easier to believe that I was an ordinary human who'd been experimented on than to believe I was... something else.

"Um, duh," Tonio replied, in that same casual tone. I realized he was chewing gum. My world was falling apart and he was just sitting there chewing gum. Then he said, "Who do you think my dad was?"

The meaning of his words hit me like a physical blow. "Oh, my God. Oh, my *God!* You're one, too?"

He looked away from the freeway for just a second, his nose wrinkled and his brows furrowed like I'd said something super offensive. "Way to be rude about it."

I ignored his hurt expression. He didn't get to be a drama queen when he'd been complicit in this for all these years. "So you're saying *Grandpa* was an alien? Does that mean all of us are aliens? Julian and Rolando and Cristina, too?" I hadn't considered this before. Even after I'd figured out I was part alien, I hadn't thought about how those parts had gotten into me. What had happened to Lola? Had she been abducted? The thought made me feel sick.

"No, those three are human. Mom's first husband was their dad. When she got remarried, she had us."

"*Married?* She was married to him? Lola *married* an alien?!" I screamed. Tonio's window was down, and I heard my voice echo off the tall buildings outside. He glared at me and rolled the window up.

"You're being an asshole, Lee," he said. "My dad was a nice guy."

I spluttered wordlessly. *A nice guy?* He was Anesidoran! He was an *alien* from a planet whose species was currently in the process of invading us and kidnapping our youth to form a super army, and Tonio was saying he'd been a "nice guy"? It took all the strength I had to rein my temper in. At last, I said, "You guys told me he was a bus driver in Manila."

"That was Mom's first husband." When I glared at him, he added, "Besides, that's not what we *originally* told you. You *used* to know the truth. We only told you that after... the incident."

I bristled. So this was another thing that they'd taken from me when they'd wiped my memories. Who I *was*. Fury swept over me again, as strong as it had when I'd heard Mom say those words on the webcam. "But why?"

"You were really upset. You were making problems."

I blinked rapidly. "Problems? Like what?"

"I dunno, man. I was in college at the time, if you'll remember. I wasn't around for most of this shit. No one ever listens to my opinion, anyway. Mom and Rosie and Phil run the show. They said this is what they're doing, and that's what they did."

Anger coursed through me. I'd been maintaining Shailene's form pretty well up until now, but the fury bubbling through my veins was making my skin tingle and pulsate. I had to close my eyes, focus on my breathing in order to keep my own appearance from slipping out. "Tonio. What was 'the incident'?"

He shifted in his seat. "Lee, I don't think—"

"Tonio, please."

My voice, unfamiliar in my own ears, threatened to break. He seemed to soften at the sound. Finally, he exhaled, his shoulders slumping. "Okay. You want to know? I'll tell you. But remember, I wasn't there for most of it, so I don't know all the details. I'm sure you figured out by now it had to do with that Shailene girl."

I nodded, finding I couldn't get words to form in my mouth.

"Well, it didn't have anything to do with the fact that you guys were an *item*," he said quickly. "You know Rosie doesn't give a shit about that. I never met her, but you talked about her a lot, and we'd all figured out you liked her from the way you were mooning over her that year. But someone apparently missed the memo, because I guess some technician got a hold of her or something. Like I said, I don't know the details. Rosie wouldn't tell me. I had to kind of piece it together from what she wouldn't say. I always thought it was weird, though, because they're not supposed to make contact with humans who are close to us. But—"

"Wait a minute," I interrupted, swatting his bicep with my open hand. "Are you for real here? Do you hear yourself? So you're saying it's okay for these aliens to *abduct* and *experiment* on humans as long as they're not people we know?"

He rolled his eyes. "It's not like that. There's been reforms and shit, I dunno. You know I don't like to get involved in politics. Besides, it doesn't involve us. Our family declared neutrality. The treaty—"

"*Neutrality?* Do you hear yourself, Tonio? How can we be fucking *neutral* when there's stuff like this going on?"

"Laura," he said, his voice severe—more severe than I'd ever heard out of Tonio, "this war is as stupid as every other war going on on this planet right now. It's no stupider than the shit going on in the Middle East, or the shit going on with North Korea, or with Russia, or anywhere else. War affects everyone. The only way ordinary people get by is by staying the hell out of it."

My blood felt like it was going to boil. Literally boil. I could physically *feel* my blood pressure surging. I clenched my teeth, pain shooting through my gums into my sinuses.

Tonio glanced over at me sidelong. "You're not going to stay out of it, are you?"

"No," I said firmly.

"Laura—"

"They have my big," I said.

His eyebrow rose. "You sure about that?"

"Yes, I'm sure. So obviously your *neutrality* treaty isn't as important to them as it is to you. And besides," I added, "there are others. Janice, and Shailene's friends. I can't just leave them." He made a noise and I glared at him. "Don't you care about what happens to humanity? Do you really want to just sit back and let everybody be enslaved to some kind of... alien overlord?"

"Well, I mean, depending on how the election turns out in November, that might be preferable."

"Tonio!"

"I'm just saying. I get you have noble intentions, Lee, but you need to be careful. I don't think you really understand what's going on here. You're not going to be helping anyone if you turn it into *War of the Worlds.*"

I didn't respond.

He exhaled noisily through his nostrils. "Fine. All right. So where am I taking you?"

"The Anesidoran base."

Tonio shook his head and drummed his fingers across the steering wheel but made no comment. He turned up the music and we rode in silence apart from the throbbing bass from the radio for a couple miles.

As we passed the City limits, and tall buildings gave way to houses and then the trees and grass of the foothills, I finally dared to speak again. "Tonio, who's Andronicus?"

He sighed. "My dad's youngest brother."

It didn't feel like a surprise, not after everything else I'd learned tonight. I nodded, trying to ignore the stone-like weight in my stomach. "Your uncle."

"Yeah. We're not exactly close, though."

Part of me wanted to know more—like how my grandfather had met Lola, or what had happened to him—but I couldn't bring myself to ask. Not now. I was still too hurt and too angry. I'd have to get answers from my family at some point, but not tonight. Tonight, I just needed to get Ana back. That was all that mattered.

"So, do you have any kind of plan as to what you're

going to do when you get to the base?" Tonio asked.

"Yeah, but you probably won't like it."

He pressed his large lips together until they formed a thin line. "Probably not. But I'll help you anyway. That's what family's for. And we owe it to you, after the way everyone's been lying to you for the last six years."

I quirked my head at him. "You mean that?"

"Yeah," he said. "Listen, Laura. What happened to you in eighth grade... I thought it was messed up. You were really upset. You didn't want to just forget. But when I tried to argue with Mom and Rosie about it, you know how they get. And then you seemed like you were better afterward, and I thought, I dunno. Maybe it would be okay." He sighed. "But then your dad came home yesterday and it was like it was happening all over again. I could hear him and Rosie and Mom all arguing, and I thought... this is bullshit. You're old enough, Laura. They can't keep running your life."

I didn't say anything, but I smiled at him, my eyes stinging. He glanced away from the road, smiling back at me.

"Okay, so," he said, "what's the plan?"

<h1 style="text-align:center">– Chapter 15 –</h1>

I didn't really have good directions for Tonio past the little town Shailene and I had stopped in earlier, but Tonio knew his way from there. He drove down one long, narrow gravel road after another, each more remote and less actual-road-seeming than the last. Finally, he turned onto an unpaved driveway marked by a rusty old sign reading *Private: Do Not Enter.* A short way down, the road was blocked with a tall gate flanked by chain-link fencing topped with barbed wire.

"Oh," I said. I hadn't thought about this. There'd been no chain link the way Shailene and I had traveled, but that route was decidedly off-road. "Maybe we should try going around? I know that fence doesn't completely circle the base."

"Nah, it's fine," Tonio said, putting the Oldsmobile in

park and opening his door. "You've gotten to show off your powers, but I haven't had a chance to give you a taste of mine."

"Your—come again?"

He winked and trudged over to the gate, sizing it up. Then he squared his shoulders and stepped forward.

I started to cry out—that gate could be electrified, and I didn't want him to shock himself—but the noise died in my throat as Tonio passed through the metal.

Seriously. Just *passed through it.*

He walked up the drive a short way to where a box with a digital display on it stood—obviously designed to work from the inside, preventing intruders—and pressed his hand to the screen. A second later, the gate rolled open. It must be designed to recognize Anesidoran DNA, like the one I'd used earlier.

Tonio strolled back to the car, looking pleased with himself.

"You're freaking Shadowcat," I said when he opened the door.

"Yup," he replied.

"So, what, are you telling me that Stan Lee is an Anesidoran or something? Is that the deal with all these superpowers from comic books?"

"I dunno. Let me know if you figure that one out," he said, grinning as he turned the car back on and continued up the drive.

The dirt drive wound its way precariously up the hill that the base was built into. It was narrow, and its lack of shoulder made me nervous. Tonio's boat didn't exactly have the best turning radius in the world. But I reminded myself that big trucks like the one Shailene and I had stolen somehow made it up this road without a problem, and tried to still my pounding heart.

At the top of the hill, the big door to the loading area was still open. Fear shot through me at the sight of it, and for a minute I thought, *What the hell am I doing? I got away from this place, and now I'm running right back to it.* But I didn't have a choice. I couldn't go back now.

Andronicus stood at the top of the dirt track, peering at us with narrowed eyes. The cut on his head had already faded into a thin, crusty scab. He must have seen us coming, realized who it was when Tonio was able to open the gate. He looked irritated, but not combative. I refused to meet his gaze.

"Tonio," he said once we'd parked and my uncle had opened his car door. "I assume Rose filled you in on the pandemonium into which your niece has thrown this facility?"

"Hey, Andre," Tonio said casually, kicking the heavy driver's door of the Oldsmobile shut. "Yeah, sorry about that. Laura went a little crazy." I bristled, climbing out of the car but standing behind the open passenger door like a shield, and tried not to glare at him.

"I don't believe the council is going to accept 'she went a little crazy' as an excuse," Andronicus replied through gritted teeth. "Not when negotiations are as strained as they are. There will be repercussions. Your line is in violation of the neutrality clause of the treaty."

"Yeah, well, I should point out that your severe lack of chill probably made things a lot worse." Andronicus looked like he was going to protest, but Tonio cut him off. "Don't worry about it, though. We got Laura home and I brought this one back for you." He gestured to me, and I nervously closed the passenger door, letting Andronicus see me.

His eyebrow flew up, and he looked me up and down. I shot him as convincing a glare as I could, trying to channel Shailene's inner bitchface.

"That one," he repeated, an unreadable note in his deep voice. "She just came with you?"

Tonio shrugged. "What can I say? I can be very convincing." He put his hand up to his mouth and added in a stage whisper, "Laura had a little something to do with it."

He winked.

I felt my face turn fifty shades of scarlet, and I glared at Tonio. He laughed, and I realized that my reaction—on Shailene's face—probably provided just the confirmation Andronicus needed for *that* insinuation. He nodded, gesturing two sentries forward. Both carried the same weapons I'd seen earlier. They grabbed my arms with their free claws.

"Do not let her out of your sight, even for an instant," Andronicus barked. "Put her directly on the transport ship. The lead technician aboard the *Okeanos* is waiting for her."

The sentries pulled me forward, squeezing my arms painfully with their vice-like pincers. I didn't dare look back at Tonio; I didn't want to give anything away to Andronicus. But fear still gnawed at me, and I struggled to not shoot one last glance at him. I didn't know what I was getting into, whether I would see my uncle again.

They dragged me back into the base I'd left only hours before, through the storage room with its maze of boxes and crates. Many of these had been upended. They lay on their sides, lids off and packing grass strewn across the concrete floor. The mad search for Shailene and me had made a mess of the facility.

The metal balcony overlooking the docking area had two staircases, each across the wide space from the other.

The sentries led me to the closest, prodding me down it with a weapon to my back. It was narrow and rickety. I tried not to look down as we descended, and was glad to have my feet on solid ground again. Two of the three space shuttles I'd seen the sentries loading with boxes earlier were gone now. The sentries steered me toward the last remaining one, and my eyes widened as I realized how much bigger it was up close than it had seemed when I'd looked down on it earlier. It was about the size of a commercial jet, but wider and squarer, with wings that folded into themselves to take up less room in the hangar. Spaceships always seem so shiny and flawless in movies, but up close, this one had some visible wear on it. Dings, discoloration—the sort of things you'd see on an older car that had several hundred thousand miles on its odometer. This ship had seen more than one takeoff and landing, and that made it seem more real somehow.

This ship was going into space. And I was going with it.

I looked down at my feet as the sentries marched me up the gangplank and aboard the ship. The back area was a cargo hold, where the storage crates I'd seen the sentries loading earlier were being stowed. The hold took up about half the ship's length. Beyond it was a door leading to an airplane-like cabin with rows of seats. Most of these seats were filled with sentries, but near the front of the cabin, I saw a familiar dark head with neatly-gelled hair. Damien. My eyes bored into the back of his skull.

Ana wasn't with him. For a moment, my heart leapt into my throat. Maybe I'd been wrong. Maybe she wasn't here after all. But by the same token, I didn't see any other humans on this transport ship, and there'd been people in those cells upstairs.

She must be aboard the Anesidoran mothership, wherever that was. I couldn't risk it—I had to make sure.

"Sir," one of my guards said in their weird language, approaching Damien. "We have the last Striker in custody."

Damien stood and turned, his eyebrow quirked in surprise. He looked me up and down appraisingly. I glared back at him.

"Right. I'll take care of her. Thank you," he said, and the sentries saluted and left us. I looked at Damien in surprise. I hadn't ever heard Andronicus thank a sentry. From my experiences with them, I didn't know if the sentries even had enough brain power to appreciate a *thank you.*

"You've been a slippery one, Striker Peterson," Damien said, flashing me a grinful of those too-white teeth. "I was beginning to think we were going to have to forget about bringing you back to Nibiru with the others."

I didn't know how to respond to that. What would

Shailene say? I settled for a glower and, "Sorry to disappoint."

He laughed and gestured me into the seat beside him, and I sank into it, positioning myself as far away from him as I could—which, considering how narrow these seats were, wasn't far enough.

"Strap in," he said, indicating the crisscrossing seatbelts on my chair, a lap belt and a five-point harness like on an aerobatic plane. "We're going to be taking off soon."

I buckled myself in with sweaty fingers and looked around the cabin. A moment later, Andronicus appeared in the doorway to the hold, looking damn smug. "The last Striker," he said as he approached us, a hint of amusement in his smooth voice. "The council will be pleased. Though I don't know if they'll be pleased enough to overlook all the trouble you and Miss Clark caused us earlier."

"What, do you want an apology?" I snipped.

Andronicus sighed. "It will be a pleasure to get you aboard the *Okeanos* and have your inhibitor adjusted."

"Oh, you don't like it when your slaves talk back to you?"

He gave me a withering look and turned to Damien. "I've had about enough of this one. Can I entrust her to you?"

"Yes, sir."

The deferential way he spoke to Andronicus made fury blaze inside my chest all over again. I couldn't believe Ana had ever fallen for this jerk and his fake nice-guy act. *"Oh, I like animals"*—what a joke. He'd been playing her to lure her into the Anesidorans' trap. Guilt that I hadn't been there for her, hadn't figured it out soon enough to warn her, washed over me once again.

Just make it to the ship, Laura. Get to the ship, get away from Damien, and rescue her. That was all that mattered. Never mind that I had no clue how I was going to do that. Somehow, hot-wiring a space shuttle seemed a bit more daunting than stealing that delivery truck had. But I'd cross that bridge when I came to it.

The ship began to vibrate, and the lights over our heads flashed and dimmed. We were taking off. I half-expected a flight attendant to appear at the front of the cabin and start going over safety procedures with us, but of course there was no one. The ship just silently shuddered to life.

Through the small windows, I could see the massive hangar door start to swing open, revealing the dark night sky and a hint of moonlight. The ship rumbled forward, its wings unfurling as it moved. It rolled down a platform far shorter than an airport runway, but apparently long enough for an Anesidoran craft, because a moment later the shuttle was in the open air, rising up over the hillside like a bird.

I gripped the arms of my seat with white knuckles and clenched my teeth. We were ascending quickly, the lights of the City spreading out beneath us like a glittering Christmas village set. Everything grew smaller and smaller as we continued to rise, and the force pressed me painfully down into my seat. Clouds wisped their way between us and the City, and I squeezed my eyes closed, terrified of getting any higher. The shuttle shook and rattled, and then—

Nothing was holding me down except the seatbelt and harness. It was bizarre, like I'd been thrown into a pool of water, and everything in me was trying to float away. Outside the windows, everything was dark; but then the ship turned, and the massive blue orb of the Earth came into view, terrifying in its enormity. The straps of the harness chafed against my shoulders, restraining me. Then there was a beep, and my weight returned in an instant. The sudden jolt made me nauseous, and I closed my eyes again, trying not to puke.

Beside me, Damien laughed. "Artificial gravity. You get used to that," he said almost cheerfully.

I didn't respond. I kept my eyes closed and focused on keeping my dinner down.

He laughed again. "We'll be docking soon, don't worry."

My nausea had only just started to subside when the shuttle began to rock again. I opened my eyes to see that we were approaching an enormous vessel—like, the size of a Star Destroyer in *Star Wars*. This must be the *Okeanos*. The Anesidoran mother ship.

I craned my head, looking through the various windows in the sides of the cabin. We were still close to Earth. The *Okeanos* must be orbiting the planet like the International Space Station. How had they managed to keep this a secret for so many years?

The shuttle grew closer to the *Okeanos* until it blocked all view of everything else, swallowing us up like some kind of ocean-dwelling predator. I squeezed my eyes closed once more as the ship rattled and jolted.

It felt like an eternity, but then, at last, we were still. In the rows behind me, I could hear sentries getting to their feet, unbuckling their seatbelts and unclasping their harnesses. I stayed riveted to my seat until I no longer felt like the world was spinning around me and it seemed reasonably certain that I probably wouldn't throw up.

When I opened my eyes, Damien was standing over me. "There, not too bad, right?" he said.

"Just take me wherever the hell we're going," I snapped.

He led me back through the cargo hold, down the gangplank and into the *Okeanos'* docking area. I looked around myself in alarm. So far, my exposure to Anesidorans had been limited to just sentries, apart from Damien and Andronicus (and, you know, my whole family). I'd seen the anatomy charts in the doctor's office back in the base, but that still hadn't prepared me for this sight now. Dozens of creatures milled around us, unloading the crates from the other two transport ships docked alongside the shuttle we'd just disembarked: minotaurs, centaurs, cyclopes, all sorts of sort-of-humanoid-but-not-quite creatures that I recognized from Greek mythology. Two small satyrs and a tall, broad, green-skinned woman bustled past me, not even glancing my way as they moved to unload the shuttle's cargo hold.

I wasn't sure whether to be amazed or terrified.

Damien followed my gaze and said, "The sentries are the only ones who can cloak themselves to appear human. The others have to stay aboard the ship. At least, until negotiations are completed. A.k.a., never," he muttered under his breath.

Outside the transport ship, Andronicus was talking to a broad, muscular cyclops and an otherwise human-looking person, both in a uniform. "The technician is waiting for her on level two," he said as we passed.

"Sir," Damien said, nodding his head—but not saluting him, I noticed. Whatever Damien and Andronicus' relationship was, they must be something close to equals.

Damien led me out of the docking area and onto an elevator. He pressed a button, and the doors swished quietly shut. I gripped the railing, still not quite over my bout of motion sickness from the brief trip through space.

Damien watched me, a bemused expression on his face. He seemed to hesitate, for just an instant. Then he said, "You feeling okay, Laura?"

- Chapter 16 -

"Excuse me?" I wasn't sure I'd heard him right. But he just smiled that frat-boy smile of his, not even batting an eye.

"You might have fooled Andronicus, but that's only because he's not good at reading other people. I could tell right away you weren't Striker Peterson. Your body language is all different."

"Um, that's creepy, analyzing our body language," I said. Then I shook my head—still Shailene's head. I wasn't about to give up this cover yet, even if Damien did see right through it. "But if you knew who I was, why didn't you say anything?"

"I wanted to talk to you," he replied. "I've wanted to talk to you since yesterday, when you ran into us outside Beta. That's when I realized that Ana's little was one of the grandchildren of Xandros the Great."

I blinked at him. "Excuse me?" I said again.

He cocked his head. "You don't know about your grandfather's legacy? He's a hero to the Anesidorans. Especially for people like us."

"People like us," I repeated flatly.

"Yeah, you know. Hapas. Mixed. Part human."

I pursed my lips. So, Damien was part human. And, evidently, part Asian like I'd initially suspected. Unless he made a habit of throwing the word "*hapa*" around under false pretenses. I wouldn't put it past him, human(ish) trash fire that he was.

"Look, I don't care about any of that," I said slowly, trying to keep my voice even. He was grinning at me like he expected me to be his friend just because we were both part Anesidoran. Well, I had news for him: It wasn't going to happen. "Where's my big?"

"Ana?"

My teeth crunched painfully as I ground them. "Yes. Ana. I know she's on this ship."

"Yeah. She's with the other test subjects on level four." Each syllable hammered into my head like a spike. She was here. She was here, specifically, to be experimented on. He'd just admitted it, like it was no big deal. Like this was the Beta house and we were having a mixer. Whatever, right?

Before I could stop myself, I whirled on him, grabbing him around the throat with a speed and strength I didn't know I had—like Shailene had grabbed the sentry back at the base. I slammed him bodily against the elevator wall just as the door pinged cheerfully open behind me.

"Take me to her. Now."

I DIDN'T LET GO of Shailene's form, not until Damien opened the door to the small room and I saw Ana sitting at a round table, reading something on a tablet. She looked up, quirking an eyebrow at me. I shot a glare at Damien, and he nodded, closing the door. He'd agreed to stay outside while I talked to her. Once the door was latched, I relaxed, my skin rippling as I morphed back into myself.

"Laura!" Ana said in surprise.

I rushed forward, throwing my arms around my big's shoulders. The tears I'd been trying to hold back all day finally started pouring out. "Ana, I'm so sorry," I sobbed. She hugged me back, patting my shoulder. I pulled away, looking her over. She didn't seem to be hurt, but after what had happened to Erikka, what could have happened to Shailene, I wasn't sure. "Are you okay?" I asked.

She stared up at me, her dark eyes round. "I'm fine. Are *you* all right?"

I nodded, sniffling and looking around the room, already trying to think of how we were going to get out of here, get away from Damien. He bizarrely seemed to think I was on his side—maybe we could use that to our advantage. "Don't worry. I'm going to help you escape. I won't let them do anything to you."

She tilted her head to the side. "Laura..."

"I'm so sorry I let this happen, Ana," I said. "It's all my fault. I shouldn't have left you alone. I should have told you."

"It's not your fault, Laura. I can understand why you wouldn't have wanted to tell me something like this. You couldn't have known that I—"

"No, it's unforgivable," I interrupted. "I promise I won't keep any more secrets from you. We just have to get you out of here, and then I'll tell you everything."

"But, Laura—"

"I knew that Damien guy was bad news from the beginning. I should have warned you. I shouldn't have left you alone with him. I never should have let him do this do you. I—"

"Laura!" Ana broke in. I stared at her in surprise. Her expression was weird. She almost looked offended. "You're not letting me talk."

I flushed and put a hand over my mouth. "I'm sorry. Go ahead."

"Laura, I don't know what you think is going on here, but I think you have it all wrong. Damien hadn't done anything to me."

My jaw dropped. Flabbergasted, I said, "Um, he abducted you and brought you aboard a space ship. Don't you remember?" I balked, wondering if they'd done something to her memories like they'd done to mine. Oh, God, what was I going to do if that was the case?

Ana shook her head. "He didn't abduct me. I came here by choice."

I blinked, moved my mouth soundlessly, then blinked a second time. "*What?*"

She nodded.

"But why?"

"Damien told me about the Anesidorans, and... I wanted to help."

"You wanted to *what?*" I came around the table, crouching in front of her and looking up into her face. She'd been brainwashed. She had to have. This was absolute insanity. "Ana," I said, incredulous, "they're *aliens.*"

She quirked her head. "You're part Anesidoran."

I gaped. "You know?" As soon as I said it, the answer seemed obvious. "Let me guess: Damien told you."

"Yeah. And he's part Anesidoran, too. So you don't have to hide it from me. I want to help you guys."

I jumped to my feet. "Okay, there are about a million things wrong with that sentence. First of all, there is no '*you guys*'. I may be part Anesidoran—through no choice of my own, remember—but I am not on their side." I started to pace around the small room in agitation. "Secondly, why would you want to help them? They're alien invaders. They're trying to take over our planet. They're kidnapping innocent people and experimenting on them, turning them into... into..." I struggled to come up with the right word, but there was no delicate way to put it. "Into freaks!"

She peered at me in confusion. "Laura, that's not true. I thought you would know, since you *are* Anesidoran..."

"Know what?"

She chewed on her lower lip, like she wasn't sure what

to say. "They're not *invading* Earth. They're trying to come home."

"What?"

She nodded. "Laura, Anesidorans are from Earth originally. They're human."

- Chapter 17 -

"That's impossible," I said immediately. There was no way. That had to have been some kind of bullshit excuse Damien had given her to try to win her over.

The door opened behind me. "It's true," Damien said, coming into the room and shutting the door behind himself.

I glared at him. "Eavesdrop much?"

He rolled his eyes. "You were yelling. And besides, someone obviously needs to explain this to you. No wonder you've been tearing up the Peninsula, ruining half our operations." He shook his head. "Didn't your mom ever tell you about your own family?"

"My parents have been a little reticent with me," I snapped. "But it's not important. None of this changes the fact that Anesidorans have been kidnapping kids all over the world for the last century, trying to force them into a life they don't want. Trying to force them to become their army."

"That's not true," said Damien. "The abductions were stopped decades ago—by your grandfather, Laura. Xandros the Great."

"You keep saying that," I said. "It's a little creepy. What, was he like a king or something?"

"He was a prince."

That stopped me in my tracks. Seriously? Now I was supposed to believe that I was not only part alien, but apparently part alien *royalty*? Are you freaking kidding me here?

"Laura, hear Damien out," Ana said, looking at me in concern. "Please. Whatever you think is going on here, I think it's just a big misunderstanding." She took the tablet she'd been looking at and handed it to Damien. "Here, show her. Maybe if she knows the whole story, she'll realize why I came."

Damien met her eyes, his expression changing—softening, sort of. "Okay," he said, taking the tablet from her. He turned to me. "Like Ana said, Laura: Anesidorans weren't originally from Nibiru. We used to live on Earth. We were humans, but we were born different. Genetic mutations made us stronger, just like they say in the comic books. We're all over ancient mythology—they used to call us demigods. In the old stories, we were heroes." He sighed. "But then things changed."

He swiped a few times on the tablet, then handed it to me. Some kind of animation was playing on the screen, a CG simulation showing planets moving through space. "Have you heard of Planet X before?"

"Before three days ago, you mean?" I looked up from the tablet. Damien was pacing around the small room in a circle. "Yeah, here and there. It's kind of a tinfoil hat conspiracy, right? Some kind of doomsday planet on a collision course with Earth."

"That's a bit of a bastardization, but it's not completely off base. Nibiru is on a highly elliptical orbit. It takes thousands of years for it to make its way around the sun, but there are periods every few millennia where it passes close to Earth. The last time was about three thousand years ago." He reached over and tapped something on the tablet. The video skipped to another CG sim. "As you can imagine, a celestial event like that... it didn't just pass by peacefully. It brought horrible cosmic storms, meteor showers, you name it. The weather changed, and crops failed. Things on Earth had already been changing for a while, anyway. Culture and religion was evolving, and more and more people were distrustful of superhumans—demigods, Anesidorans, whatever you want to call us. Perception was shifting. Our powers were starting to be seen as a curse rather than a blessing."

On my screen was a depiction of what looked like an ancient Greek village. As I watched, the sky turned dark, and balls of fire started cascading down. It reminded me of a video we'd watched in World History class in high school about the destruction of Pompeii. The ground shaking, buildings collapsing, roofs caving in, people screaming. It wasn't pleasant.

"When Nibiru passed, it made for the perfect opportunity for the non-Anesidoran leaders to scapegoat us. They made the people believe we'd caused this. We'd opened Pandora's Box and brought this on humanity. They started hunting us. They cast us out."

I looked up from the video on the tablet, which had switched to some kind of cheesy movie depiction of a battle, complete with a close-up decapitation. It was clearly designed to manipulate the viewer emotionally, but I wasn't buying it. This was just an Anesidoran recruitment video with a Hollywood budget. It was propaganda.

"Okay," I said, "so *if* I decided to believe you that any of this happened—and I'm not saying that I do—how exactly did the Anesidorans get from Earth to Nibiru? Even if it was as close as the moon, this was three thousand years ago. People didn't exactly have space age technology back then."

"You know we all have different powers. Some of us have the power of teleportation. When Nibiru was on its closest approach, they helped the rest escape."

"Oh, come *on*, Damien," I said, rolling my eyes. "Interplanetary teleportation? Seriously?" Even after everything I'd seen this week, that one was a step too far. There was no way. That was impossible.

"He's telling the truth, Laura," Ana broke in. She'd been so quiet, I'd almost forgotten she was still in the room. "I've seen it."

I stared at her. There were so many layers to that sentence, I couldn't even begin to dissect it. What did she mean, she'd *seen* it? I wanted to press her on it, demand to know the details—How could she have seen it? And when? How long had she known about this? And if it had been a while, why had she kept it from me?

But then she looked at me, her expression earnest, and a wave of guilt washed over me. I had been keeping secrets, too, and for probably the same reason. There was no reason to blame her any more than I should be blaming myself, yet here I was, letting that pettiness consume me again. It was like the remorse of the past day had made no difference. I still wasn't listening to her, still wasn't trusting her. That had to stop.

I let out a weary sigh. "Okay. So the Anesidorans escaped from Earth to Nibiru. I'm with you on that. But why did they—you—uh, *we* want to come back? Why try to return to a planet that hates us so much that its inhabitants drove us away?"

"Nibiru's not a great place to live, Laura," Damien said. "I haven't spent a lot of time there, but the time I have, I've hated. The weather is out of control. The orbit is so elliptical, there are periods of boiling hot and freezing cold. The animals that lived there already were monstrous. We had to fight to survive there. We still are, even with our advanced technology. We can't stay there. It's not where we belong. We belong on Earth."

I looked back down at the tablet, not really focusing on the images on the screen.

"The Return started a little over a hundred years ago. The royal family thought that if we could make the rest of Earth like us, they would help us. Obviously we see, now, that that was a bad idea. But a lot has changed over the last hundred years—on both sides. You know that. Look at life a hundred years ago, two hundred. You know there were a lot of bad ideas running the show."

I shrugged. I couldn't argue with that, much as I wanted

to.

"Your grandpa was the one who changed all that. He was the crown prince of Nibiru, but he abdicated when he became involved with a human woman—your grandmother. He wanted things to change. He didn't believe that turning the whole world into Anesidorans by force was the way to get them to accept us. He believed in diplomacy. At his urging, the royal family and the high council changed their policy. Now they only accept volunteers who want to help strengthen human-Anesidoran relations by unifying our genetics. There have been no abductions for the last thirty years because of him—"

I'd been leaning against the round table, but I jerked upright at those words. "Now *that*? That *is* a lie," I snapped, cutting him off.

"It's true!" he protested.

"No, it's not. I have proof of that one." I prodded him in the chest with my index finger. "Shailene and the other Strikers. All the kids at Bayview University. They weren't *volunteers*, Damien. They were kidnapped."

He grimaced. "Laura, I hate to be the one to tell you this," he started.

But I never got to hear what he was going to say. Because the door behind us opened abruptly, and standing in the doorway was Andronicus.

And behind him were my parents.

- Chapter 18 -

"So sorry to interrupt," Andronicus drawled, "but it's time for this charade to come to an end."

I looked past him at my parents standing in the stark, white hallway. Somehow, seeing my mom and dad here, on a freaking *spaceship*, was too much for me to take in. It was like a damn parent-teacher conference aboard the Death Star. "What are you guys doing here?" I asked.

"They're taking you home," said Andronicus. "For, I hope, the last time. You have caused more than enough trouble for one lifetime, young lady."

"Andre, shut up. I'm the one who chews my daughter out, not you," my mother said, looking haughtily at Andronicus. Then she turned to me. "And as for you—you are in big trouble, young lady. You know how much stress I've been under this week. And you pick now of all times to find your rebellious streak? When we've got a houseful of company? Now your poor grandma has to entertain them by herself, and at her age."

I couldn't believe my ears. I was so angry, I didn't even care that we were airing our dirty laundry in front of my big and a practical stranger. I marched out into the hallway to meet her head-on. "You have got to be freaking kidding me. Do you even hear yourself? I just found out that you people have been lying to me about who I am for half my life, and all you care about is what the cousins think? And, for real, you know Lola is more than a match for them, so nice try." She'd married an alien, after all. If I'd had any doubt about my grandma's demonic powers before, it had been wiped away now. If any of them crossed her, she'd probably body slam them like The Rock or something. My mom didn't get to play the guilt card there.

"You should have come to us if you had questions," Mom argued.

"I didn't get a chance!" I shouted back.

"Okay, that's enough," my dad said, inserting himself between us. He glanced beyond me to Ana and Damien. Apparently, he did care about saving face, even if I didn't. "We can talk about this when we get home."

I laughed hysterically. "Are you kidding me? Why should I go anywhere with you liars?"

"You don't have a choice," Andronicus interrupted. "Now, I want you off my ship in the next five minutes, or else you're going to be reporting to the Anesidoran high council and I don't give a damn about family ties. You can rot on a pillory for all I care."

My dad reached for my arm, but I ripped it away from him. "I'm not going anywhere until I get some answers."

Andronicus closed his eyes and gritted his teeth. I'd done the same thing a million times before, and my stomach clenched in revulsion at the thought that this could be a family trait. "Five minutes, Rose."

He stormed down the hall. My mom turned to me, and I could see the gears turning in her head, switching tactics. She was going to try to say something soothing to calm my temper, but I was ready for her. I broke in before she even got a chance to open her mouth. "Who are you people, anyway? It's like you're total strangers. You locked a huge part of me away inside myself. Don't you care about me at all?"

"Of course we care," my mom protested, her voice filled with hurt. "Why do you think we did it in the first place?"

"To control me," I spat.

"No. To help you. Laura, you don't remember what it

was like after... the incident. You were wild with grief, with anger. There was nothing we could do. You said you didn't want to be Anesidoran anymore. We couldn't erase that part of you, Laura, but we could suppress it. It seemed like that was the only thing we *could* do to help you. We were desperate. We were willing to try anything."

"It was wrong. It was fucked up."

My mom's eyes glistened with tears, but she wouldn't let them spill over. She squared her shoulders, looking at me ferociously. "I see that now. But that's hindsight, Laura. Nobody knows intrinsically how to be a perfect parent. All that mattered to me was making you stop hurting."

"You shouldn't have erased me, you should have *stopped* them. You're Anesidoran royalty! You *could* have stopped them. You let them take Shailene," I snarled.

"Laura, your mom couldn't do anything to stop it," my dad said then, putting his hand on my shoulder. I brushed him off. "The I.G.A. is too dangerous, especially for people like her. People like you. We didn't dare reveal our family to them."

"What the hell does the I.G.A. have to do with it?" I asked. "They *rescued* Shailene. The Anesidorans were the ones who took her."

My dad narrowed his eyes in confusion. "What are you

talking about?"

"She doesn't know, sir," Damien said over my shoulder.

I whirled on him. "What don't I know?"

"It's what I was trying to tell you just now," Damien said. He seemed hesitant, but I was about ready to throttle the information out of him, and I was pretty sure he knew it. He took a step away from me. "We didn't abduct Striker Peterson, or any of the other Swordsmen. It was the I.G.A."

My breath caught in my throat. "What?"

"It's true, Laura," my dad said. "Believe me, I know. Remember, I used to work for them."

"But why? I mean... How?"

My dad let out a scornful snort. "The government figured out a long time ago that superpowered humans made the best soldiers. They made an illegal deal with an Anesidoran separatist faction—a black market arms dealer. They combed the local middle schools and high schools, looking for teenagers with certain physical characteristics. Anyone who stood out on their sports teams or had high scores on their physicals in gym class. They don't even think of these kids as people. That's why they call them 'lab rats'." He crossed his arms. "They facilitate the abductions themselves."

"But I don't understand," I said. "The I.G.A. are the ones who *saved* Shailene."

"Of course they did," sneered my dad. "If you want someone to fight for you tooth and nail—be willing to sacrifice their very lives for you—what better way than to create a debt? If the experiments believe that the I.G.A. are their saviors, they'll be more than willing to use their powers to help the agency in their battle against the ones who did this to them."

His words from before—"*The I.G.A. are not your friends*"—echoed in my ears. Oh, my God. How could I have been so stupid?

"Is that why you left, Dad?" I asked in a small voice.

He didn't meet my gaze. "I wish I could say that was why, Laura. But..." He glanced at my mom. She put her hand on his shoulder, as if to let him know it was all right. Dad sighed and nodded. "About twenty years ago, the I.G.A. shifted their tactics. They discovered that some Anesidorans were... *reproducing* with humans, to use their terminology. Having kids together, like..." He swallowed. "Like your mom. And you."

"And me," Damien put in cheerfully.

"Right," said Dad. "I'd been dating your mom for a while at that point, but I'd only recently found out that she was part Anesidoran. The I.G.A. put me on an assignment, to take out a—a *subject of interest.* Up until that point, I'd believed the lies they were spinning about the war. I believed, like you did, that we were under invasion, that the Anesidorans wanted to destroy us. But after I found out about your mom, my perceptions started to change."

"He didn't know at first who I was," Mom explained. "But when we got engaged, I told him. And that's when I found out he worked for the I.G.A.—he wasn't supposed to tell anyone where he really worked, so he always just said he was a government contractor. But obviously there was a bit of a conflict of interest there when he learned the truth." She sighed. "I introduced him to my parents, and my dad told him about his work on Nibiru-Earth relations."

"Rosie's father made me realize that what the lines the I.G.A. had been spinning us weren't true. He was a reformer, a diplomat. But the I.G.A. wasn't interested in his diplomacy. Shortly before my last assignment, he was assassinated. The government tried to manipulate it to appear as though an Anesidoran separatist faction had been behind it. There were a number of groups on Nibiru who didn't want to stop the abductions, who didn't want to give up until every human was like them, so it wasn't outside the realm of possibility. But I was starting to have my doubts by then."

"I didn't believe that he'd been killed by an Anesidoran, and neither did your grandma," Mom said. "We had a feeling the I.G.A. was involved. The whole thing was just very suspicious."

"And then I got put on this assignment," Dad said. "They told us this subject was a terrorist, a high-ranking Anesidoran who'd abducted hundreds of humans to be experimented on. They said she was the mastermind behind a plot they'd uncovered to attack the U.N. building. Whoever she was, she was dangerous, right?" He shook his head in disgust. "Imagine my surprise when I discovered that the 'subject of interest' was your mother."

My mouth opened involuntarily. "Mom?"

"Yeah," my mom said. She turned away, pacing the hall in agitation. Even after twenty years, she was obviously still really upset. "They'd killed my dad, and now they wanted to kill me. Because they realized that half-Anesidorans were stronger than regular lab rats. We had powers beyond what the I.G.A. and their traitor technicians could invent in a lab. So we had to go." She shook her head. "My dad had done everything in his power to keep Tonio and me a secret. All my life, I'd never understood why. But then they found me, and it became all too clear."

I felt sick. "So what happened?" I asked, dreading to

find out the answer.

"When I figured out that Rosie was our mark, I had to warn her. I tried to slip away from my partner, but he was too fast. He figured out what was going on. And..." He trailed off, looking at his hands.

My mom ceased her pacing and put her hand on his shoulder. "It wasn't your fault, Phil." To me, she said, "Phil and your dad got into a fight. Phil was trying to get his gun away from him, and... it went off. The bullet went clean through his partner, and grazed your dad as well. Fortunately, his wounds weren't severe."

Dad stared off at nothing. "I didn't want it to work out that way. But I had to protect your mom. So I went back, filled out a report. I said we'd been successful in taking out the mark, but that Jon had gotten killed in the crossfire. I asked for a dispensation for psychological reasons, and I got it. It took almost a year, but I got it. By then, your mom had gone into hiding. After I left the I.G.A., I changed my name and joined her. We moved around a bit before settling down in Everett. You probably don't remember; you were only two or three when we moved to the ranch."

"And we've hidden from them ever since." I shuddered, folding my arms and looking down. "Why didn't Tonio tell me any of this?"

"He doesn't know most of it," my mom said. "It's safer for him that way. He was only eight years old when Dad was killed. We've tried to keep him in the dark about the I.G.A.'s involvement as much as possible. I don't think he even knows about their lab rat program. The more he's able to live his life like a regular human, the better. And the same thing goes for you, Laura. We would never have told you if you hadn't gotten mixed up in it all. Twice," she added bitterly.

"I really screwed up this time," I said in disgust. "After the way I blundered in, the I.G.A. must know all about us now." I broke off. "Dad, you and Janice knew each other before. Does that mean she...?" Did she know what had happened to my dad all those years ago? What was going on within her agency? She'd taken Shailene in after the abduction, but had she been a part of the kidnapping to begin with?

My dad sighed. "I don't know. I doubt it, though. Most of the worker bees at the I.G.A. don't know what's really going on. A lot of them are regular humans, like I was—I told you the truth before, Laura. I wasn't an abductee." He shook his head. "But if word got out, the lab rats might rebel."

So Janice probably didn't know, but she'd started to piece it together. That's why she'd had that file about my dad in her backpack. I wondered if she'd figured out who I really was yet? If the I.G.A. knew my mom was still alive—if they found out about me, or Tonio—they'd come for us.

They might even send the Strikers for us.

I felt like I was going to throw up. I'd been wrong all along. I'd believed that the Anesidorans were behind the abductions. It had made so much sense. After all, there'd been the jail cells I'd seen earlier at the base when I'd rescued Shailene; but I realized with a jolt that I hadn't actually seen anyone in those cells. I'd just assumed. They'd fit my narrative, and I'd accepted it without question.

There was just one thing that didn't make sense. Slowly, I said, "But if the Anesidorans only take volunteers now, why are they kidnapping the Strikers? And brainwashing them like this?"

"We are not kidnapping anyone," a smooth, deep voice said. I looked up to see Andronicus striding down the hall. "And it's been more than five minutes. It's time for you to go."

I ignored that, pushing past my parents and storming right up at him. "Oh, yeah? Then what do you call it? All the Strikers have disappeared one by one, and I saw them leave with you." I whirled on Damien. "And you, Mr. Simple."

"That was part of our new peace negotiations with Earth. The ones you seem to be so eager to completely destroy."

"Peace negotiations?"

"We called the I.G.A. out on their secret lab rat program," Damien explained, coming back out into the hall. "They agreed to return the Strikers to us in exchange for some other concessions."

I blinked two, three times. "Excuse me? They just *traded* you the Strikers? Like they're a goddamn sports team?"

Andronicus looked past me to my mother. "Rose..."

"Don't you bring my damn mother into this," I snapped. "Look, I agree that what our government has done to you guys is fucked up. But in case you forgot, the Strikers are still people. You can't just take them without asking their permission."

"We don't have time for this. Damien, escort them off the ship."

"Yes, sir."

I ripped my arm away when he reached for it. "I'm not going anywhere with you."

"Oh, but you are," Andronicus snapped. "And I don't want to hear one more word out of you, or I can't guarantee that your girlfriend will make it back to Nibiru in one piece."

My heart stopped. Just totally stopped. It felt like a brick wall had slammed against my chest. "What do you mean, my girlfriend?"

"Andre, you can't make threats like that," my mother snapped, giving him a warning look. "You have your Strikers. Let us take Laura back home in peace."

"*What do you mean, he has his Strikers?*" I shrieked. I'd left Shailene back at Gam-Lam. She'd been safe. It had only been an hour or two at this point. She had to be safe still. She had to be.

My mom pulled me away from Andronicus, trying to talk soothingly. "Shailene called us earlier, Leelee. That's how we knew you were here. She told us what you'd done, and said she wanted to surrender."

"WHAT?"

Andronicus rolled his eyes and turned away. Clearly, he was done with me. "Damien, get them to the transport shuttle."

"No!" I screamed, fighting against Damien as he grabbed my arms. "Let go of me! Damien, I swear to God—Ana, do something!" But he'd closed the door to Ana's room—her glorified prison cell. I'm sure it was locked from the outside. The Anesidorans weren't any better than the I.G.A. They'd tricked her, just like I thought. I twisted around, looking at my mother imploringly. "Mom," I begged.

"I'm sorry, Laura," she said, avoiding my eyes.

I screamed and fought, kicking and pulling as hard as I could. But Damien was too strong. No matter how I struggled, I couldn't get away.

I was trapped.

- Chapter 19 -

The three of us sat alone in the otherwise empty cabin of the transport shuttle. Damien had left to go find a couple sentries to escort us back down to Earth. I'd screamed and cried myself hoarse, and for nothing. There was nothing I could do.

I stared down at my hands sullenly.

"It'll get better, Leelee," my dad said, patting his hand on my shoulder in that annoying way of his, where he smacks you firmly enough to reverberate through to your ribcage and doesn't seem to notice.

I set my jaw and didn't respond.

On the other side of me, my mom said, "Laura, this was Shailene's choice to make," in what I was sure she considered a reasonable voice.

"Oh, yeah, definitely," I replied. "The fact that her mom

and all her closest friends had been taken definitely didn't coerce her or impede her judgment in any way."

Mom sighed and rolled her eyes.

"Did you give the the note, hon?" my dad leaned forward to ask across me.

"Oh, I forgot," my mom said. "Here, Laura. Maybe this will make you feel better." She shifted in her seat and pulled a piece of lined paper out of her pocket. She handed it to me, and I unfolded it. I didn't recognize the handwriting, but I recognized her words.

Laura,

I know what you're trying to do. I know you didn't tell me because you were trying to protect me. But I can't just stay here alone while everyone I care about—and that includes you—is in danger. The other Strikers are my family. I can't just leave them. If only one of us comes out of this safe, I want it to be you. Please. Please stay safe.

Shailene.

Hot tears bit at my eyes as I reread the note over and over. "I'm sorry," I said at last, "is there a bathroom on this thing?"

"In the back, in the cargo section. I'll show you," my mom said, starting to unfasten her seatbelt.

"No," I said—or snarled, really. "I'll find it myself." I pushed myself out of my seat and hurried to the back of the shuttle, my vision watery.

The bathroom was larger than the pathetic closets you get on commercial airlines. It was more like an actual single-stall bathroom. Big enough that I was able to sink onto the cool tile floor, not even caring what kinds of germs I was sitting in. I pressed my face against my knees. I thought I'd cried myself out, but apparently I was wrong.

After a few minutes, a soft tapping came at the door.

I ignored it.

Another knock, and then I heard my mom say, "Laura, please open up."

"Or what, you'll phase through it like Tonio?" Bitterly I stood up and unlocked the door. Mom stood on the other side, looking oddly small.

"No. That's not my power," she said sheepishly.

She came into the bathroom, and I shut the door behind her. "What is your power, anyway? Besides your standard Filipina-mom-guilt powers?" I glared at her, but she didn't rise to the bait. She closed the lid to the toilet and sat down on it, crossing her ankles.

"You know," she said simply.

I looked down at my feet, not responding.

She sighed. "Laura, I understand how you must be

feeling."

"Really, Mom?" I shook my head. "I'm super sure you do."

She made a noise of frustration and crossed her arms. "You're not giving me enough credit. Do you think that my life's been any easier than yours? How do you think I felt when my father was killed by I.G.A. agents? How do you think I felt when they tried to force your father to assassinate me?"

Guilt gnawed at my chest, but I ignored it. "So the I.G.A.'s fucked up. You won't get any argument from me there. But you don't think that what the Anesidorans are doing is fucked up, too?"

"Of course it is," Mom said, splaying her hands. "No one is in the right here. But all that's going to happen if we get involved is that it will tear our family apart, put us in the crosshairs. The I.G.A. has been after me for years, and crossing the Anesidorans would put your father in danger. There's no side we can take that doesn't risk one of us. The only way to protect you and the rest of our family is to stay neutral."

That damned neutrality again. I leaned against the wall. My eyes felt swollen from the crying, and the cool tile was soothing against my lids. "Mom," I said, my voice hoarse and ragged. "How would you feel if it was Dad up there in that ship right now? Or Tonio, or Julian, or Rolando, or Cristina?"

She didn't answer for a long time. Finally, I opened my eyes to look at her. She was staring down at her own feet now, at the chipped red polish on her toes. When at last she spoke, it was in a whisper so quiet I could barely hear it.

"...I'd bust the ship apart to find them."

I crouched down in front of her, looking up into her face. "But you're asking me to just leave Shailene and Ana behind." I could feel my face burning, but I still doggedly added, "You know who Shailene is to me, don't you, Mom?"

"Of course I do. I remember eighth grade."

I put a hand on her foot. "You want me to go through that again? Because I'll tell you what, I'm not letting you block my memories again. That might work on a thirteen-year-old, but I'll die before I let it happen now."

"I know. I wouldn't do that to you again, Leelee." She ran a hand through my hair, like she used to when I was little. For just an instant, I closed my eyes and let myself pretend that I was small again, when everything was easier.

But maybe things had never actually been easier. Maybe the hard memories were just missing.

I swiped at my eyes with the back of my hand. "I can't

go back, Mama," I said. "I can't leave her."

A beat passed, then she stroked my hair again. "I know."

I stared at her, unsure I'd heard her correctly. "What?"

She stood, pulling me up with her, and drew me into a hug, pressing her nose against the top of my head. "I know, Laura."

I LEFT THE bathroom, still sniffling, and went back to the cabin where my dad was strapped into his seat, ready for takeoff. A couple of sentries sat noiseless on either side of the cabin, not seeming interested in anything other than ensuring I didn't leave the shuttle.

I sat next to my dad, buckling my harness.

"Where's your mom?" he asked.

"In the bathroom still. She said she wanted to stay in there until we're back on the ground so she doesn't have more... trouble." Apparently she'd been pretty badly airsick on the way up. That hadn't surprised me when she'd told me—her motion sickness was so bad, it made mine look tame. She needed to take Dramamine even on long car trips.

My dad looked at me and patted my knee. "It'll be okay,

sweetie. We'll get through this."

I nodded but didn't say anything.

The transport ship vibrated and hummed, rumbling forward into the airlock where it would disengage from the *Okeanos*. I closed my eyes, trying not to be overwhelmed by the queasiness.

My dad squeezed my hand as we broke away from the mothership and our bodies lifted from our seats once again. There was the same nauseating weightlessness, followed by the jolt as the artificial gravity kicked in.

"I'm never going to get used to that," I said aloud.

We sat in silence, me breathing slowly through my nose trying not to be sick, my dad patting my hand reassuringly, until the ship re-entered the Earth's atmosphere.

As we were landing, Dad asked, "I wonder if your mother's doing okay?"

"I'm fine," I said. "And I managed to not throw up this time."

Then my body shifted into that of my mother's.

"Surprise," Mom said with a grin.

At least, I assume that's what happened. I didn't see any of it myself. I was already back on the *Okeanos*.

- Chapter 20 -

I hurried down the hallway, taking care not to be seen. When I'd been in Shailene's form, Andronicus had told Damien that there'd been a technician waiting on the second level. That must be where she was now.

This level was broken into odd sections, each separated by large bulkheads. It almost seemed like more than one ship had been patched together to make this part of the *Okeanos*. Moving through this level was slow-going. I couldn't shift and didn't have the time to find someone whose form I could steal that wouldn't lead to me being caught. But I wasn't completely helpless. Before I'd left the transport shuttle, I'd seen Shailene's electrified nightstick laying in an open crate amid a ramshackle assortment of items I guessed had been taken from the Strikers. I clutched it to my chest now.

I took the hall in sections, hiding behind corners looking around to make sure no one was coming, methodically making my way through level two until I came to another large bulkhead. This one had a symbol on the door that reminded me of the symbol we used on Earth to indicate hazardous materials, interlocking circles in the shape of a triangle. That made me nervous, but I'd already made up my mind that I needed to check behind every door. I craned my neck, looking around for any signs of sentries. Then I crept forward, pressing my hand to the keypad. The door slid open.

This door opened on a long hallway with windows in both walls. It reminded me, for some reason, of the airlocks you see in science fiction movies—one door on one end, and one on the other, with a decompression area in the middle. The door at the end of the hallway had a porthole in it. I crept over to it and peeked inside to make sure the room was empty.

Well, the room *wasn't* empty. But there were no Anesidorans inside as far as I could see. So I unlocked the door and crept in.

It was some kind of lab, almost completely dark. Small lights blinked on a computer console in the center of the room, and pinpricks of stars shone through the large window to my left. This part of the ship was facing away from the Earth, so the massive blue globe that was visible from other parts of the *Okeanos* was nowhere to be seen.

No, the main source of light in the room was coming from the thirteen glass tubes on the wall directly in front of me.

The tubes were tall, glowing bright blue. Each tube held a human figure suspended, as if they were floating in water, though there seemed to be no liquid in the glass. Their eyes were closed, their faces blank and peaceful. I only vaguely recognized most of them from the night I'd scrolled down the Swordsmen Athletics webpage, but the two on the far left I recognized as Leah and Joanie—the first two girls who had been captured.

I walked closer, my eyes moving down the row of tubes. Involuntarily, my fingers flexed and clenched into a fist. They were all here. All of the Strikers. The twelve cheerleaders and Janice. It was like they'd been cryogenically frozen or something.

I stopped in front of the last tube, my chest clenching uncontrollably, and slowly lifted my hand to the glass. There was Shailene, her porcelain features relaxed, serene, as if she were sleeping. Her hair gently curled around her.

I was too late. If she was here, they'd surely erased her by now. Her memories would be gone again. Even if I could free her from this glass prison, she wouldn't remember me. She'd probably fight me. What was I going to do?

I rested my forehead against the glass, squeezing my eyes closed. *Shailene...*

Behind me, someone cleared his throat, and the overhead lights to the lab flickered on. "You are like a bad penny." I whipped around to see Andronicus emerging from the shadows. He'd been here all along. It was like he'd been expecting me. Maybe he had been. It would explain why I hadn't run into any opposition on my way over here. And he was right, I had set a precedent of coming back like a boomerang. Not that I was going to apologize about it.

"What do I have to do," he said dryly, "to get rid of you?"

"There's nothing you can do. Just deal with it." I gestured to the thirteen glass pods. "What the hell is this? What are you doing to them? Brainwashing them isn't good enough?"

"They are not *brainwashed*," Andronicus said, folding his arms. "We merely activated their free will inhibitors. That's something the I.G.A. installed, incidentally." He shot me a snide look.

I shot him one back. "Let me guess—leftover tech from back before Gramps did away with the abduction program? Because I know it's Anesidoran technology. You used the same thing to block my memories, didn't you?"

He shook his head, irritated. "I don't know why you are being so antagonistic. We did it to help them, Laura. We need to take them back to Nibiru, per our agreement with Earth. Activating the inhibitor was the easiest way to do it, and the best way to ensure they weren't injured in the process. The Strikers have been fighting us for years at your government's behest. They're dangerous warriors."

"Bet you're real glad to have them on your side now, huh? Even if you had to wipe their brains to do it." We stared frostily at each other. "So what's with these tubes?"

"These will keep the Strikers in stasis until the Nibiru high council has determined their fate. Deliberations could take months. After that time, they'll more than likely become part of the Anesidoran army."

"With or without the help of the inhibitors?"

He exhaled wearily. "I don't know, Laura. The council will decide that. It's not my place."

"Andronicus, come on," I pleaded. "They're *people*. Surely you must see. You're destroying their lives."

"No more than the I.G.A. did to begin with."

I threw my head back in frustration. "Andronicus, you know this is wrong. The Strikers should be told the truth and allowed to make their own decisions, like... like your test subjects." Like Ana, as much as I didn't want to accept that. "You're acting like you've got the moral high ground because the I.G.A. started this, but you're still turning thirteen people into zombies."

"All's fair in love and war. That's an Earth proverb, Laura. Surely you're familiar with it."

I stared at him. He really wasn't going to see reason, was he? So I'd have to do it my way. "All right, Andronicus. All's fair? Then this is fair." In a quick motion, I ripped out Shailene's nightstick and charged him. I thought for sure surprise would give me the upper hand, but he dodged my blow with expert skill, and returned with one of his own.

We lunged and parried. Andronicus was bigger, and he was trained, but anger made adrenaline course through my veins, and that lent me speed and strength I didn't know I had. I charged at him, punching again and again, but he was always a fraction of a second ahead of me, dodging my blows repeatedly.

He twisted away from me, lifting his hands. His skin rippled the way mine did when I transformed, swirling a kaleidoscope of colors like it had in my dream. But his form didn't change; instead, a ball of red light began to grow in the space between his fingers, crackling and pulsing. He hurled the orb in my direction, and the bright red lightning I'd seen him use against the Strikers crackled around me. I flung my arms up, blocking the energy with Shailene's nightstick. The lightning cracked, blinding, arcing off the blue electric sparks of the weapon and dispersing.

Andronicus charged at me again, and I braced myself for the force of impact, but he rushed past me to the tube just behind me. I whirled in horror just in time to see him fling down a switch, disengaging the pod. Steam erupted from the tube as its glass lid opened.

I froze, unwilling to move. "What are you going to do to her?" I asked, terrified. He'd opened Shailene's stasis tube. He'd threatened her before, but I genuinely thought he'd been bluffing. But I knew he knew that I would do anything to keep him from hurting her, and that knowledge made him reckless—and me desperate.

She opened her eyes, looking around herself in confusion.

Andronicus smirked. "It's not a question of what I'll do to her," he said. "It's what she'll do to you. Striker Peterson?"

She blinked, then looked at Andronicus with cool, expressionless features. "Yes, sir?"

He pointed at me. "Take her down."

In an instant, she was on me. Reflexively, I flung the nightstick up, blocking her attack. "Wait, Shailene—no!" She dodged away from the nightstick and lashed out with her leg. I tried to turn away, but I was too slow, and her foot connected painfully with my side. I doubled over, leaping away from her as she kicked at me again. "Shailene, please! I know you're in there somewhere. Don't you recognize me?"

She lunged at me again, knocking the nightstick out of my hand. I dove after it, but she was faster. She brandished the weapon, crackling with blue electricity, and faced me, every muscle poised to strike. She was like a mouse trap, ready to snap.

I backed away from her, my hands up. "Shailene, come on... please... I know you're in there. I know you remember me. You have to. Even after what they did to us before, erasing our memories... we both still remembered. Deep down. I know your memories are there."

The words seemed to make her hesitate, just slightly. She cocked her head to the side, her eyes blank but a hint of confusion playing at her expression.

"Shailene," I implored. "It's Laura."

"Striker Peterson," Andronicus snapped. "Finish her. Now."

She advanced on me, raising the nightstick to bring it down over my head. I cringed, looking away, but the blow never came.

I looked up, my heart pounding in my ears. She stood over me, her arm raised, but she didn't move. The room was silent except for the electricity crackling and pulsing off the nightstick. Why wasn't she moving? It was like she was frozen in place.

"Striker Peterson!" shouted Andronicus.

Her face was as blank as a mannequin's. But in the corner of her eye, there was the slight glimmer of an unshed tear.

My heart broke at the sight of it.

I didn't think. I just moved. I took one step forward, closing the distance between us, brushed that tear away with my thumb, cupped my hand against her cheek and pressed my lips against hers.

The world exploded in sharp agony and blinding light.

WE WERE RIDING our bikes down the gravel road leading to my parents' ranch. It had become a daily ritual at this point, the two of us racing each other from the science classroom to our bike racks as soon

as the bell rang, then pedaling our bikes the mile and a half from school back to my house. We'd become inseparable over this last year, closer friends than I'd been with anyone, even Charlie. We'd watch movies together, and I'd introduced her to my favorite video games. We'd have sleepovers and sing along to '90s boy bands and get up at the crack of dawn to feed the chickens. We shared all our secrets together.

Well, almost all our secrets. There were two that I'd kept closely guarded from Shailene, that I didn't dare open up to her about. The first was being Anesidoran, something my mom had forbidden me from telling anyone my whole life. That was an easy secret to keep. I kept it from everyone. I had practice.

And the second secret? Was that I was falling for her. Big time.

That secret was getting harder to keep every day.

Shailene turned the corner through the open metal gate first, gliding up the short paved driveway from the road to our house and dumping her bike on its side in the front lawn. I was just a second behind her, and she laughed as I hit the brakes, skidding to a stop.

"I won again," she said, putting her hands on her hips with a grin.

"Of course you did," I said, panting. "You're like a superhuman or something." It was true. The only way I could keep up with her was if I tapped into my Anesidoran side. On my own, I was no match for her. When we'd had our physicals in P.E. this year, she'd gotten the

quickest speed out of all the girls in our class.

"Winner gets to choose what we do," she said.

"Let me guess: Hang out with the goats?"

She flashed an enormous smile, the one that had been making my heart loop-de-loop in my chest every time I saw it. "Of course," she said. "I have to see my Violet!"

In addition to the chickens that my mom raised for their eggs, my dad kept goats, sheep and alpacas on the ranch. Shailene had fallen in love with the goats the first moment she'd seen them. Her favorite was a doe named Hyacinth, and she'd been ecstatic when, this spring, the doe had given birth to a little kid we'd named Violet. Every day when we got home from school, Shailene had to check in on them.

I followed her out behind our house, to the big pasture that the goats were grazing in. She called out to them, and the whole herd lifted their heads and came bounding over, Violet hopping ahead to reach her first. "That's my girl," she said, laughing as Violet nibbled at her fingers.

I found myself staring, as I often did. I couldn't help it. It was getting almost pathetic, the way I was mooning after her. Even after all these months, I still wasn't sure whether she even liked girls or boys, or both. She hadn't mentioned being interested in anyone, and I hadn't dared. I knew she knew about me being gay—the whole school knew it. It had never really been a secret. But I also knew it wasn't exactly common, and I had developed a talent at keeping my feelings to *myself, especially around girls of questionable orientation.*

We sat in the grass, chatting about nothing while she held Violet in her lap. It was Friday afternoon; homework could wait until Sunday. We had the whole day to ourselves.

As the sun started to set, Lola came out into the backyard and called across the grass to us. "Dinner in fifteen minutes, Leelee. Is Shailene eating tonight?"

"No, ma'am, I have to get home," Shailene called back. I always laughed at the way she called Lola and my parents "ma'am" and "sir." They'd all told her to call them by name a long time ago, but she couldn't seem to drop the habit. "My parents expect me to be polite," she'd say from time to time. I didn't think it was impolite to call your best friend's parents by their names, but I didn't push it.

As Lola shuffled back into the house, Shailene looked at me, an odd expression on her face. "I probably ought to get going," she said. "I don't want my parents to get mad again."

I raised my eyebrows. "Again?"

"Er, I mean..." Her face colored, and she avoided my gaze. "It's just..." She rubbed her hand across the back of her neck. "I don't know. Laura, what did your parents say when you told them you liked girls?"

I blinked. The conversation had taken a sudden turn in a direction I hadn't expected before. "Not much. They didn't seem super surprised by it. I think they got the message pretty early on, when they noticed that all the fairytale books I was drawing in my free time always had two princesses instead of a prince."

She smiled almost wistfully. "I bet that was nice, huh?"

"Yeah, I guess. Shailene, are you okay?"

"It's fine," she said.

It didn't seem fine. It seemed the opposite of fine. Her face seemed to be getting sadder every second.

She pushed Violet off her lap. Together, we led the goats back to their barn, as we did every night before dinner. When we shut the barn door, she looked at me, seeming to steel herself before she spoke. "Laura, I want to tell you. I like girls, too."

My heart jumped, beating so quickly I could barely feel the separate beats. "What?"

"Yeah. I noticed it... a while ago. But I haven't told anyone else yet."

"Oh," I said, trying to sound casual. Truthfully, I didn't really know what to say. No one had ever come out to me before. Now, to have my best friend and the girl I'd been hopelessly crushing on for the last eight months tell me she was gay, too? I was completely speechless.

"Um," she said, her voice shaking a little bit, "so, when you like a girl... how do you tell her?"

My face was on fire. She had to see it. Even in the pink light of the setting sun, she had to see it. "I don't know, actually," I said sheepishly. "I, uh, I never actually have."

"Oh," she said in a small voice. "Really?"

"Yeah. I usually just... kind of act like an idiot around her until she stops hanging around with me. So far, anyway." Like what was happening right now. I really, really would have liked the ground to open up right then and there and swallow me whole, in fact.

She nodded thoughtfully and didn't say any more. I walked with her back to where we'd left our bikes earlier. She picked hers up, wheeling it down the driveway.

I watched her for a minute; then, impulsively, I said, "I'll walk you to the corner."

"Oh. Okay."

The two of us walked in silence down the road. If I'd been paying attention, I would have noticed that she was walking much slower than usual. It took us almost five minutes to get from my house to the corner. I was too preoccupied with my thoughts. I wanted to ask her. Wanted to tell her. But I was absolutely terrified of things changing between us.

Finally, I managed to mumble, "So, like... Do you have a girl you like?"

She didn't meet my eyes, but she nodded her head in a nervous, jerky motion that made her dark hair bounce against her shoulders.

"That's cool," I said lamely.

There was a stop sign at the corner, where our drive met the main road into town. She paused there, seeming suddenly shy and unsure of *herself.*

"Well, I'll see you tomorrow, I guess?" I said.

"Yeah. Tomorrow," she answered. She stood there for a moment, not looking at me. "It's you," she said suddenly. I stared at her, taken aback, uncertain how to respond. "You're the one I like."

My mouth fell open. I couldn't find my breath. "Seriously?"

She nodded, avoiding my gaze.

I swallowed, feeling myself break into a grin I couldn't quite control. "I... Me too."

She looked at me hesitantly. "You too?"

"I mean... I... You're also the one I like."

She stared at me, looking as unbelieving as I felt. Then she propped her bike against the metal pole of the stop sign and came over to me. Before I could react, she'd leaned in, kissing me softly on my lips. I didn't even close my eyes, I was so surprised.

Her kiss was gentle, and sweet. She tasted like cherries. It made my heart beat erratically, my face go flush.

It was everything a first kiss should be.

She pulled away after just a second, her cheeks and ears beet red. But she was smiling. So was I, uncontrollably.

"Bye," she said, getting on her bike and pedaling away.

"I CAN'T SEE YOU ANYMORE, LAURA."

She wouldn't meet my eyes. She kept fiddling with her hair, pulling it forward over her ears, tugging at the ends nervously as if to make sure it stayed in the same place. She was trying to hide that bruise on her cheek. She'd put makeup on it to cover it up, but it hadn't done any good. Shailene never wore makeup, and whatever she'd used didn't quite match her skin tone. If anything, it made it stand out more.

I wanted to ask why, but I already knew the answer. It seemed mean to make her say it when I knew she didn't want to.

"Can't we still hang out?" I asked, my voice barely louder than a whisper. I couldn't bring myself to look at her, so I stared down at the janky picnic table we were sitting at. I ran my finger over a name that had been carved roughly into the brown paint. It was getting dark, and the park down the street from Shailene's house was deserted apart from the two of us. "You're my best friend, Shai. It's okay if that's all we can be."

She shook her head. "I'm not supposed to talk to you anymore. At all. Not even at school."

"But... that's not fair!" I protested. "They can't do this to you, Shailene. Isn't there anything we can do? Maybe we should talk to my parents—"

"No!" she cried. Her eyes were wide and scared-looking. "I can't. I just—I'm sorry, Laura. Please. I'm sorry."

"O-Okay," I stammered.

She jumped up from the picnic table and hurried away from me. I watched her go, too stunned to feel anything but numb. I should have seen this coming, I supposed, after everything she'd told me about her parents. But I'd never really believed anyone could be that horrible to their own kid. I'd been spoiled, I guess.

From the picnic table, I could see her turn onto the street and keep running down the sidewalk. Dark shadows filled the space between the trees, but when she ran past a fat oak, I thought I saw a pair of shadows detach themselves and drift after her.

I stiffened, watching them. It was two men.

Without thinking, I ran after them. That was exactly what my parents had always told me not to do in a situation like this—I was to pull out the clunky old cell phone they'd gotten me for emergencies and call 9-1-1—but I didn't want to let Shailene out of my sight. I just went into autopilot.

By the time I'd reached the park's entrance, they'd already caught up with her. I burst through the trees just in time to see the bigger man grab her.

"Stop!" I screamed, sprinting after them with the heightened speed I'd spent my whole life trying to conceal.

Shailene struggled, trying to fight the man off, but he was too strong for her. I was about to launch myself at him when a bright blue light flashed in my eyes, and then I saw just what this man was.

He was Anesidoran.

There was a noise like an explosion, and Shailene slumped limply forward. "No!" I shouted in Anesidoran, launching myself at the man and grabbing his arm. "What are you doing? She's my friend."

"Stay out of this, little girl," the other man said, pulling me away from them and clamping a hand over my mouth. "Unless you want to join her." He seemed to be a normal human—what was he doing here with this other man? And what did they want with Shailene?

"Wait!" the Anesidoran shouted. "Don't touch her. She's under Anesidoran protection."

The human man laughed. "Do you really think I give a damn about that?"

"I know you don't. But there will be trouble for us if you interfere with her. Just leave her."

I managed to jerk my jaw open enough to bite down on the pad of the man's hand. He cursed and shoved me away from him. "That does it," he said, reaching for his gun. I screamed and hunkered down.

"I said, leave her!" the Anesidoran man boomed. There was a bright flash and an explosion like thunder. For a horrified instant, I thought it was a gunshot—that I was done for.

But then the smoke cleared, and the two men and Shailene were gone.

I'D RUN ALL *the way home, bursting through the door hollering at the top of my lungs. I'd run all the way home, bursting through the door hollering at the top of my lungs. My mom had called Uncle Andre as soon as I'd told her what had happened, demanding an explanation. But he didn't have one. Whoever these men were, the Nibiru high council knew nothing about them.*

"It's the I.G.A.," my dad said, his voice dark.

"You have to do something!" I screamed. I screamed it over and over, my heart pounding like a drum, my brain a panicked, hysterical mess. There had to be something they could do. If anyone could stop this, it would be my parents, or Lola, or Uncle Andre. I hadn't spent a lot of time on Nibiru as a kid, but I'd been there enough to know that no one could mess around with my family. We could stop this. We could save her.

But there was nothing we could do.

"WE CAN'T CROSS THEM," my dad said firmly, for what had to be the hundredth time. "They're too dangerous."

I sat in the dark at the foot of my bed, my eyes bloodshot, my face stained with tears. "What's going to happen to her? Is she ever going to come back?"

Dad shook his head. "She'll come back. But when she does, she won't be her anymore. She'll belong to the I.G.A. She probably won't even remember you. You're going to have to let her go, Lee."

I wanted to laugh in his face at that. She was my best friend. She was more than that. She was the most important person in my whole life. How was I supposed to just let her go?

MEMORIES BLURRED AND RUSHED, whirling together in a tidal wave, slamming into me. Screaming. So much screaming. Fighting and yelling and desperation and anguish and grief, because no matter how I tried, there was nothing I could do.

And then it all went blank.

Chapter 21

The pain evaporated, and I slowly became aware of warm lips on mine, fingers tangled in my hair, pulling me closer, holding me desperately. Then we broke apart, and my eyes snapped open. I gasped for air.

Shailene was holding me, as much confusion on her face as there was on mine. The bright light of the lab had gone dim again, punctuated with flashes and pops, and around us erupted the crackling sound of electricity. I turned to look around the lab. Sparks and smoke were pouring from the large computer hub in front of the stasis tubes. Andronicus cursed violently.

"You've destroyed our network," he shouted, waving smoke away from himself.

As I realized what his words meant, a grin broke across my face. "Oh, sorry, did I fry your little brain inhibitors?"

He looked at me with cold fury. "I need to isolate this quadrant before the rest of the ship is damaged." His nostrils flared. "You've made your choice, Laura. Now you're going to have to live with the consequences."

He stormed out of the lab.

My grin broadened. "Seriously? We won? He's just letting us go?"

Shailene was looking at me oddly. She took a deep breath and said, "I remember now. I remember you. Eighth grade. Everything."

"Me too," I said, my cheeks burning. "We can talk about it later. For now, we need to get the other Strikers out, right?"

She nodded, still seeming shaken. I couldn't tell from her reaction whether getting her memories back was a good thing or not.

One by one, we moved down the line of glass tubes, opening each and helping the Strikers emerge. I watched as Shailene stopped in front of Janice's pod, shaking with relief and throwing her arms around her when Janice opened her eyes. Janice seemed taken aback at first, but as she got her bearings, she returned the hug, and I heard her murmuring reassurances quietly into Shailene's hair the way my own mom had earlier.

I was just opening the girl I remembered as Leslie's tube when there was a hard jolt. Leslie staggered forward into me, and we fought to regain our bearings.

"What was that?" Erikka asked, looking around in alarm.

"I don't know," I said, glancing over my shoulder at the smoking remains of the computer bank behind me. Andronicus had been pissed about the state of their system. What if we'd damaged the ship worse than I'd realized?

As Leslie moved to help another girl out of her stasis tube, the ship jolted again, and I saw movement out of the lab's large window. I turned and sucked in my breath just as a mechanical-sounding voice filled the air, coming from an intercom system. *"Lab One: disengage,"* it said in Anesidoran. Through the window, the main body of the *Okeanos* was twisting, seeming to move farther away from us. I remembered the impression I'd gotten that the second level of the ship seemed to be comprised of several different pieces, attached haphazardly. I realized, with sudden horror, that maybe I hadn't been wrong.

I blanched, and Shailene caught my eye. "What is it?"

"The lab is disengaging."

"What?"

Joanie rushed to the lab door, trying to turn the handle.

"It's locked."

"Let me try," I said, hurrying over and pressing my hand to the digital pad beside the handle. The screen turned red and a loud, shrill beep sounded.

"*Disengagement in process,*" the voice on the intercom snipped over my head.

I cursed and kicked the door hard. "It won't let me open the door."

"Then we can't get back to the main part of the ship," Janice said, snapping into business mode. "We'll have to find another way out. There must be escape pods. Strikers, fan out."

The other girls spread out across the lab. After a minute, Leah said, "Coach, over here. They've been launched already."

"What?" I came up behind Janice, peering over her shoulders to see. There was a small airlock where you could see clearly some kind of intergalactic lifeboat should be attached, but it was gone.

"*Life support system override activated. Three minutes remaining.*"

"Andronicus," I said bitterly. He didn't want us to escape. My knees started to shake, and Shailene watched me with concern. Hesitantly, she reached out to put a hand on my shoulder. I winced, expecting the familiar stabbing behind my eyes, but no pain came. We could touch.

For all the good it would do us now.

"So what, are we trapped?" Erikka asked, her brows knitted across her dark eyes.

"Keep looking. There must be another way. Maybe this segment of the ship can be piloted independently," said Janice.

"I don't see how, with that computer destroyed like that."

"We're dead," I whispered. I couldn't believe Andronicus could be this spiteful. When my memories returned, fleeting glimpses of the man I'd known as Uncle Andre had returned as well. He'd never been a warm man, or particularly close with our family; but he wasn't bad. He'd tried to help when Shailene had first been captured. I couldn't believe that he was really the sort of person to leave his own flesh and blood to die out in the vacuum of space. Even after all the trouble I'd caused him.

But I had caused him a *lot* of trouble.

"*Two minutes remaining.*"

"This is all my fault," I said, hot tears stinging my already painfully-swollen eyes.

"No," Shailene said firmly, taking my hand in hers and

squeezing it tightly.

"It is," I said, turning to face her, our fingers still interlaced. "I ruined everything, blundering in like this. And now you're going to die."

"Laura, it's okay," she murmured.

"How is it okay?" I cried.

"Because we have each other," she said, in a voice only I could hear. And I knew then—we had our memories back, and it was a *good* thing.

We had each other, in the end.

"One minute remaining."

The other cheerleaders were standing at the window, watching as the *Okeanos* moved farther and farther away from us. The airlock that had connected the lab to the ship was drifting away between us, spiraling slowly into the blackness. I tried not to focus on my fear. There was no point in panicking. It wouldn't help, not with so little time remaining. I placed my left hand on the glass of the window, my right still tightly clasping Shailene's, and looked at our translucent reflections staring back at us.

Over my reflected shoulder, a shadow glimmered into existence. One second he wasn't there, and then, abruptly, he was. I gasped, turning around.

It was Damien.

And now I knew what Ana had meant when she said she'd *seen* it. This was Damien's power.

"Strikers," he said breathlessly. "You need to come with me—now."

"Damien," I said. "What are you doing here?"

"There's no time. Just come on. I'll probably end up court-martialed for this, but... not every Anesidoran is without morals, Laura."

I blinked in surprise. The Strikers all looked at me, and then to Janice. I could tell they weren't sure whether they should believe him. But you know what? I did. Against all odds, I really did. And regardless, we were staring death in the face. Whatever Damien wanted to try, it had to be better than suffocating in the vacuum of space.

I nodded at Janice, and she nodded at me. I glanced at Shailene, still clutching my hand tightly in hers. She nodded, too.

"Let's go," I said.

Damien held his hand out to me. "There's no time to take you all individually," he said. "We're going to have to try to go all at once."

"Can you do that?" I asked.

"I've never tried," he said. "But I know it's been done. It's how we got to Nibiru, after all. So I'll just have to give it my best shot."

I nodded, taking his hand with my free one. "I trust you, Damien."

He beamed, as if my approval was the most important thing in the world to him. I realized in that moment that he sort of reminded me of a puppy. No wonder Ana liked him so much.

We all clung to each other, forming a human chain, then a circle, wrapping arms around each other to make the connection as small and tight as we could. Anything to make it easier for Damien to carry us all.

"Ten seconds remaining."

"Hang on, ladies," Damien said.

I closed my eyes.

And in a blink, we were home.

- Epilogue -

It was going to be a hot day. Already now, at ten o'clock, the fog had burned away completely, and the sun was beating down like a heat lamp. The air was thick with the scent of eucalyptus trees, sweet and homey. It was only the end of March, but if the weather kept up like this, summer would be here before we knew it.

I looked down at the park below us, watching the tiny speck of a jogger running up the trail, passing a couple walking leisurely with a big, fluffy sheepdog. No one seemed to notice the two figures high above them, nestled between the flames of Firebelle Tower.

A week had passed, but I still hadn't quite come down from all that had happened aboard the *Okeanos*. I'd somehow miraculously managed to make it through the first few days of classes without passing out—though I was pretty sure I'd bombed my Public Speaking presentation. (I probably would have done that anyway, though.)

"Have you heard from your big at all?" Shailene asked from her perch amid the flames.

"Yeah. Well, not directly. But I talked to Damien last night. They'll be back on Tuesday."

I hadn't been able to convince Ana not to go, in the end. Before Damien had left, after he finished transporting the Strikers and me back to Earth, I'd pulled him aside.

"Wait, Damien," I'd said. "What about Ana?"

"What about her?"

"I mean, isn't she coming back?"

Damien hesitated, looking at me guardedly. "She already told you, Laura."

"Yeah, but things are different now. Just let me talk to her, one more time."

He looked at me like I was bonkers. "I can't bring you back aboard the *Okeanos*, Laura. That would be suicide. I'm sure Andronicus is going to figure out what I've done, but I'd rather it be later rather than sooner, you know?"

"Then bring her here," I urged.

"I can't do that." He looked at me, his expression softening. "But if you insist, I can let you talk to her." As I watched, he pulled his phone out of his pocket. He swiped a couple times, then handed it to me. *FaceTime with Bae, connecting,* the screen read. I tried to resist the urge to barf.

"Hey," I said when she answered.

"Laura!" Ana exclaimed. "Are you okay? What's going on? The ship was shaking, and then Damien left and I had no clue where either of you had gone."

"I'm fine. Damien brought me back home. He's here with me now." He leaned over and waved at her over my shoulder, and I rolled my eyes.

"Thank God," she said. "I'm sorry about what happened earlier, with your parents. I didn't know you didn't know. I feel so stupid."

"It's not your fault," I said sincerely. "I'm just sorry it all blew up in front of you."

She smiled at me, and I knew if she'd been beside me, she would have reached out to pat my arm or give me a hug. It made me feel hollow.

"What about Shailene?" Ana asked. "Is that going to be okay?"

"Yeah, it's fine," I said. "Damien got her and the other Strikers out, too. I guess"—I sighed in a long-suffering way—"I guess he's all right."

Beside me, Damien beamed, flashing his disgustingly-white teeth at me. On the phone screen, Ana grinned too.

"I wanted to make sure," I said slowly, hesitantly, "you know, maybe... maybe you might want him to bring you home, too?"

She shook her head. "I'm sorry. I made up my mind. I want to help the Anesidorans."

"Yeah, but you don't have to be... *changed* in order to help, right?" I reasoned. After all, they couldn't change everyone on Earth.

"Regular humans can't survive on Nibiru," Damien said. "They need the modifications to be strong enough to survive the climate, the amount of high-speed space travel we have to do to get back and forth between the two worlds. A regular human can only make the trip once or twice before their body starts breaking down."

I exhaled slowly. This wasn't going to work, was it? She was going and that was that.

"It's okay, little. I'll be back before you know it. The procedure just takes a day, and they'll have me stay a few days longer to monitor me, but then I can come home. I already cleared it with my professors. Well. That I'd be gone, anyway. They don't know where I'm going." She smiled, and the phone shook slightly, the image blurring from a moment before going clear again. "And then I'll be like you, right? We'll have no more secrets."

I sniffled. "I like you how you are."

"I'll still be me, Laura," she said with an incredulous laugh. I didn't look at her, and she folded her arms. "This is my choice to make. I can do with my own body what I want."

I knew she was right. But I couldn't make myself be happy about it. Even now, with her just a few days from returning, I didn't know how to feel. Would things really be the same when she got back? Everything was changing. I just wanted one thing to stay how it had been.

But I supposed that was too much to ask.

"I'm glad she'll be back soon," Shailene said now. She smiled, but I noticed she looked distinctly uncomfortable. I knew she was thinking about herself. Her own change hadn't been a pleasant, regularly-scheduled-visit-to-Nibiru-with-a-set-return-date. And that had been the I.G.A.'s doing. As uncomfortable as the thought of Ana... *evolving* was to me, she'd at least had a choice in the matter. I still felt that the Anesidorans were manipulating her, but it was nowhere near the level that the I.G.A. had manipulated the Strikers.

She stood, brushing off her bare knees and coming over to the concrete balcony where I sat. "What are you guys going to do about the I.G.A.?" I asked, watching her.

Now that Shailene and Janice knew the truth about the I.G.A., I didn't see how they could continue to work for them.

"I don't know. We've talked about it, but… it's hard to get away from them. Your dad was able to get a dispensation because of what had happened to his partner. I don't know if we qualify for one, or what we'd have to do to break away. I don't want to change my name again, and I don't want to leave the City. Maybe we're better off staying where we are, fighting from the inside."

My stomach knotted. I didn't like that, but was it really any worse than my own situation? Maybe that's all any of us could do. Fight with what we had.

I still remembered what Andronicus had said to me when he'd let us go. "*You've made your choice, Laura. Now you're going to have to live with the consequences.*" And I remembered what Damien had said, just an instant before he'd disappeared:

"He didn't want to leave you out there, Laura. Regardless of what you think of Andronicus, he's really not that way. But he didn't have a choice. He had orders. If anything were to compromise the Strikers, they had to be destroyed. The Nibiru high council was firm on that. We couldn't risk them coming back to Earth."

But we'd brought them back to Earth anyway, Damien and I. And what would the consequences be? One thing I knew for certain: I'd thrown away my family's neutrality. Whatever happened in the coming war, we'd be involved. And if the Nibiru high council wanted to punish us for what I'd done, I didn't know if there was any way I could stop them.

But I was sure as hell going to try.

"Let's not worry about it right now," I said. "The future is going to be a mess, and all we can do is face it as it comes. Let's just think about the present." Like right now—the fact that after all these years, we were whole again. No more buried memories. No more secrets, no more lies. She laced her fingers through mine, squeezing my hand, and I thrilled at the contact. It still felt unreal, that we could touch each other with no pain. That alone made everything we'd gone through worth it.

This was one change I didn't mind in the least.

We sat together quietly for a long while, her fingers laced through mine and her head on my shoulder. The sun climbed higher in the morning sky.

"Hey," I said at last. "I was thinking... My sorority formal's coming up at the beginning of May. Do you think you might... wanna be my date? Providing the world hasn't ended by then, of course."

She sat up, looking at me with her eyebrow arched. "You sure it won't give Claudia the vapors?"

I snorted. "Hey, as long as 'paramours' stay out of the upstairs area, she doesn't give a shit what we do outside the house. Besides"—I grinned—"she's not my mom."

My mom, on the other hand, had given me her blessing. My dad had been furious when he'd found out about the trick, but I think he understood why Mom had gone along with it. He just worried, for all of us. He wanted to protect us. To keep us out of the crosshairs of the Anesidorans' conflict with the I.G.A. And I appreciated it. But some things were worth the sacrifice.

This was worth the sacrifice.

Shailene grinned, her eyes crinkling adorably at the corners, making my heart skip a beat. "Then I guess I'm going to have to figure out what one wears to a sorority formal. God, I hope not a prom dress."

"You can show up in your cheerleading uniform for all I care," I said.

The two of us laughed, and she looked at me sideways. "So, Laura Clark: Is this a *date* date? Does this mean you're asking me out?"

My face flushed. We hadn't really talked about it—we

hadn't even really discussed the kiss on the *Okeanos*, actually. I wasn't sure if she remembered what had happened on the ship. "I mean, only if you want it to be," I said shyly.

She leaned close to me, her breath feathering across my cheeks, and I got the very distinct feeling that she did, in fact, remember. "I do," she whispered.

I closed my eyes, and her lips pressed against mine, gently, tentatively. Like she had the very first time, all those years ago. It was like a fairytale kiss, soft and delicate. She pulled away far too quickly, leaving me empty and longing for more. Then she looked at me quizzically, tilting her head, as if asking permission, if that had been okay.

It had been more than okay.

I cupped her cheek in my hand and pulled her in again, and I felt her laugh against my mouth. She kissed me harder, deeper, until I felt dizzy. I leaned back against the hot concrete balustrade for support, and she followed me down. The warmth of her body pressed over the top of me, her legs tangled with mine, my fingers wrapped in her hair, hers roaming across my skin in tantalizing circles. Her lips were like fire, as blazing as the sun glinting bright off the flames around us. I drank her in, letting that fire engulf me.

At last she drew away, leaving the two of us gasping for breath. She grinned impishly down at me, her hands braced on either side of my shoulders, the sun behind her head forming a halo of light that glimmered through her hair, casting her features in soft shadows. I never wanted to tear my eyes away from that face. She looked like some kind of otherworldly being, glowing like that.

And she was. We both were.

"I've dreamed of doing that for years," she whispered. "I just never realized that I was dreaming of you all along."

I pulled her down to me and kissed her again, her mouth, her cheeks—smiling as my lips brushed against the soft curve of her jaw.

"Me too," I said.

Acknowledgments

At its heart this book is really about family, so I have to start out by thanking my own, by chance and choice. You guys were very much the inspiration for Laura's own quirky family. From the beginning, this story grew out of a dream I had where we were all together in Shirley's backyard, laughing and yelling and pigging out on shrimp lumpia (the best kind!). *AND THEN THE ALIENS ATTACKED*. Haha. Thank you all for everything.

I also want to thank my sorority sisters, particularly my big, Sara, for being such an integral part of my life and this story. Too often I see fictional depictions of sororities being catty or cliquey or cultish—but for me, it was the opposite. For years, I had inadvertently surrounded myself with people who made me feel less-than and unworthy. My sorority sisters were the ones who made me see my own value, and gave me the strength to break away from those abusive "friendships" and truly find myself. Thank you all and Beta Phi!

A huge thank you to my wonderful editor, Amy McNulty, for helping me make this book the best it can be. Enormous thanks also to my audiobook narrator Adrian Mayes for being Laura's voice and bringing her to life in a way I'd never imagined before!

Thank you to the individuals who supported this book and who helped make it a reality, especially RoAnna Sylver, Claudie Arseneault, B R Sanders, Kiran Oliver, S.L. Dove Cooper, and everyone who encouraged me as I worked on the project.

And finally, thank you to my readers, for all your support and encouragement during my ups and downs over the last year, and for being so kind and patient with me while I finished this book. I hope that it was worth the wait.

About the Author

Lyssa Chiavari is an author of speculative fiction for young adults, including *Cheerleaders from Planet X* and The Iamos Trilogy, a sci-fi series set on Mars. She is also the editor of the anthologies *Perchance to Dream: Classic Tales from the Bard's World in New Skins* and *Magic at Midnight: A YA Fairy Tale Anthology*. Her short fiction has appeared in *Ama-Gi* magazine, *Wings of Renewal: A Solarpunk Dragon Anthology*, *Clarion Call: Echoes of Liberty*, and *Brave New Girls: Tales of Heroines Who Hack*. Lyssa lives with her family and way too many animals in the woods of Northwest Oregon. Visit her online at lyssachiavari.com.

Books by Lyssa Chiavari

The Iamos Trilogy

Fourth World

New World

One World

*Different World*s: An Iamos Novella

Anthologies

Perchance to Dream

Magic at Midnight